DOCTOR WHO - ENLIGHTENMENT

DOCTOR WHO
ENLIGHTENMENT

Based on the BBC television serial by Barbara Clegg by arrangement with the British Broadcasting Corporation

BARBARA CLEGG

Number 85
in the
Doctor Who Library

A TARGET BOOK

published by
the Paperback Division of
W. H. ALLEN & Co. PLC

A Target Book
Published in 1984
by the Paperback Division of
W. H. Allen & Co. PLC
44 Hill Street, London W1X 8LB

First published in Great Britain by
W. H. Allen & Co. Ltd 1984

Novelisation copyright © Barbara Clegg 1984
Original script copyright © Barbara Clegg 1983

'Doctor Who' series copyright © British Broadcasting Corporation 1983, 1984

The BBC producer of *Enlightenment* was John Nathan-Turner, the director
was Fiona Cumming.

Printed and bound in Great Britain by
Hunt Barnard Printing Ltd., Aylesbury, Bucks.

ISBN 0 426 19537 X

For Adam, Rufus and Jemima,
my most constructive critics

CONTENTS

1
Winner Takes All

'Check!'

There was satisfaction in Turlough's voice as he moved his queen into position. He had his opponent on the run now, and very soon the white king would be cornered and completely surrounded. Shadows seemed to darken over the chessboard, and Turlough only just managed to control his irritation. Why did all the power in the TARDIS have to go on the blink just when he was winning?

'Check!' he repeated crossly.

But Tegan's mind was not on the game. She was holding a torch for the Doctor as he fiddled with something deep in the interior of the console. All that could be seen of him were two long legs and a pair of wriggling feet. He emerged with a smear of dust on his cheek and a look of interest in his eye.

'It isn't a leak,' he said. The discovery seemed to intrigue more than alarm him. 'Our power's being tapped somehow.'

'Tapped!' Tegan was horrified. She had always considered the power of the TARDIS to be impregnable. The Doctor had told them that nothing could get at it. And here he was, taking the whole thing quite calmly, while the lights in the control room grew dimmer and dimmer and their energy slowly ebbed away.

'Come on!' Turlough sounded more exasperated still. All he could think about was the game, and slowly and reluctantly Tegan joined him.

'Your move,' he prompted.

The Doctor was tinkering with the controls on top of the console, only part of his attention on their conversation, when the last word of it suddenly echoed strangely in his head.

' . . . Move . . . move . . . move . . .'

It did not sound like Turlough's voice any more. It was someone he knew, he was sure, but very faint and far away.

' . . . Move . . . move . . . move . . .'

The echo died as suddenly as it had started. Tegan and Turlough did not seem to have heard anything, and the Doctor decided that it must have been his imagination. He pulled himself together and concentrated on his repairs, muttering to himself as he worked.

'Block the outlet . . . there . . . and then any minute . . . we should have full power . . .'

' . . . Power . . . power . . . power . . .'

There it was again! The Doctor shook his head and pressed his hands to his ears, so abruptly that Tegan looked up from the game.

'What's the matter?' she asked in startled concern.

'Ssh!' The Doctor silenced her with a gesture. 'I'm trying to listen.'

'What to?' they wanted to know. The Doctor had to confess that he was not sure. Turlough grinned and shook his head in mock resignation. He was always pleased with any chance of getting one up on the Time Lord, and for once Tegan sided with him. The Doctor was behaving in a rather peculiar manner. Then, instead of continuing to fade, the lights in the control room suddenly glowed much brighter. Then dimmed again. And brightened. Dimmed . . . brightened . . . As though someone – somewhere – wanted to attract their attention.

'Of course!' As usual it was the Doctor who clicked into action first.   'It's a message!'

Before they had time to pull themselves together, he leapt towards the console, throwing switches and shouting, 'Turn up the power!'

'Turn it up?' Tegan and Turlough exclaimed together. 'We're . . . We're supposed to be conserving it . . . Now look here . . .'

' . . . Here . . . here . . . here . . ,' echoed in the Doctor's head. And then the echo was moving towards one of the doors, ' . . . here . . . here . . . here . . .' The Doctor followed it, shouting commands over his shoulder.

'The photon lever . . . increase energy output . . . keep it at full . . . whatever happens . . .'

And before they could stop him or ask another question, he had flung open the door and disappeared into the corridor beyond. They looked at each other, completely bewildered.

'He must know what he's doing.' Tegan tried not to sound too worried.

Turlough peered into the dimness. The Doctor's voice came back to them faintly from the end of the passage.

'Think so?' Turlough queried dryly. 'At the moment he's out there talking to himself.'

The Doctor did indeed appear to be having a conversation with thin air.

'It is you, isn't it?' he asked the empty gloom ahead. 'We're giving you everything we've got.'

11

For a minute nothing happened. And then, just in front of him, silvery robes began to glimmer into view, and finally a face: a kind, but rather stern face. It was the White Guardian, his lips moving silently.

'I can't hear you!' The Doctor had never felt more frustrated.

All at once, as though someone had turned a volume knob, the words became audible.

' . . . Power . . . balance of power . . . at risk . . .'

The voice continued to come and go as the White Guardian glimmered in and out. 'Danger . . . extreme danger . . .' And then he was simply an echo in the Doctor's head again calling 'Danger . . . danger . . . danger . . .'

By now a thin stream of smoke was rising from the console and Tegan and Turlough watched it, mesmerised.

'What does he think he's doing?' Turlough muttered. 'Another minute and we're going to blow!'

Tegan took an involuntary step towards the door. She could not see the Doctor in the gloom of the corridor, but she called to him. Out of the blackness came a terse 'Keep back!'

The Doctor stared ahead, willing the image to reappear and prompting urgently.

'Go on! Co-ordinates galactic north six degrees . . . What's next?'

'Nine . . . zero . . .' came faintly back, as the White Guardian glimmered into view again, flickering and fitful.

' . . . Seven . . . seven . . . go at once . . . must not allow . . .'

'What? Not allow what?' asked the Doctor frantically.

The White Guardian's lips moved soundlessly for a

second, and then, very faintly, the Doctor heard, 'Prevent . . . the sign of death.' And once more it was only an echo in his head, ' . . . Death . . . death . . . death . . .'

Without warning, all the lights in the TARDIS came on again, and the White Guardian vanished completely.

The Doctor was as startled by the sudden brilliance as Tegan, but she was the first to realise what had caused it. She rounded on Turlough just as his hand was moving away from the lever.

'You've reduced the power!' she cried out, shocked. And then the Doctor was back in the room, with such a stony expression that even Turlough felt uneasy.

'I thought we were going to blow up.' he muttered defensively.

'Never – ever – touch that console again.'

The Doctor's voice was cold and cutting, and he turned his back on Turlough and began setting co-ordinates.

'Who were you talking to?' Tegan wanted to know. The White Guardian's name meant nothing to her; but if she had not been so busy asking questions and if the Doctor had not been busy telling her there was no time to explain, they might have seen Turlough's look of terror. It was clear that the name did mean something to *him*, and something that caused him extreme alarm. They never did notice, however, because no sooner were the co-ordinates set than the TARDIS lurched violently and the three of them were thrown across the room.

Tegan felt gingerly for bruises, but the Doctor seemed quite oblivious of any discomfort as he picked himself up and dusted himself down.

'Time override,' he remarked casually. 'The locking

must have been in the co-ordinates.' And then he added with sudden gravity, 'We're here.'

There was a pause.

'Where?' asked Tegan.

The scanner showed total blackness outside, and the Doctor had to admit that he was as much in the dark as the TARDIS. He did not know where they were nor what they were supposed to be doing — the White Guardian's instructions had been interrupted too soon. All he did know was that they were supposed to stop something happening. Something dangerous.

'And when the White Guardian says there's danger, he's invariably right,' he remarked briskly.

The atmosphere analyser showed the air outside to be breathable and Turlough was despatched to get two torches for himself and the Doctor.

'Make it three,' Tegan called after him. 'I'm coming with you.'

She turned on the Doctor, ready to argue, but faltered at the look in his eyes. It was one she did not often see there. The Doctor was seriously worried.

'I need you here,' he said. 'The White Guardian is sure to try and make contact again.'

'Why don't you wait, then?' Tegan wanted to know. But the Doctor shook his head.

'No time to waste. It's too urgent'.

Turlough was back in the room as he finished speaking, almost as though he had been eavesdropping.

'I'll stay, if you like,' he offered, his voice just a shade too casual.

The Doctor looked straight at Tegan.

'I want someone I can rely on. It's important.'

Tegan gave up.

'All right,' she said, resigned. 'What do I have to

do?'

Carefully the Doctor explained that she was to stand by, ready to operate the lever when the White Guardian tried to speak again. The message was vital, and his power was so badly depleted that he would need to draw on theirs to get through at all. Tegan was taken aback.

'You mean – the power drain was the White Guardian?'

'Exactly!' said the Doctor. And then he and Turlough had their torches at the ready and he was opening the main door.

'What shall I do if he tells me something important?' Tegan stuttered.

'Thank him politely.' And with a smile the Doctor closed the door firmly behind him. It was not until she was alone that Tegan remembered that she still had no idea what the White Guardian looked like. Or, indeed, who he was.

Cautiously the Doctor and Turlough felt their way forward, shining their torches into the blackness. The ground had turned out to be a wooden floor, but there was no clue as to the sort of building they were in. Odd creaks sounded from time to time, and then a scrabbling noise. The Doctor stopped so suddenly that Turlough bumped into him.

'Rats,' came his soft murmur, out of the gloom.

A minute later, the beam of his torch hit something solid ahead. It was a wall of boxes and crates, piled on top of one another and roped together.

'Must be a warehouse,' Turlough whispered. And then, without any warning, the floor suddenly heaved under their feet. Both of them reeled and almost lost their balance, and as Turlough put out a hand to

15

steady himself he had panicky visions of earthquakes and landslides. Another tremor followed almost immediately and the ground trembled again. But the Doctor had seen something interesting on the floor ahead and was bending down to examine it. When he straightened up, he held a piece of rope in his hand.

'Look,' he said, as though everything were suddenly explained.

It was not until he pointed out what was on the end of the rope, and Turlough saw the tar, that he realised what the Doctor was getting at. They were aboard a ship. A sailing ship. There was another heaving movement, but this time they automatically swayed with it. 'Getting our sea legs,' Turlough thought. And then, in the black void beyond the crates, a faint shaft of light appeared. They caught a sudden glimpse of a companion-ladder, and a figure descending it. The Doctor grabbed Turlough's arm and pulled him down behind the crates. Torches off, they squatted there in the darkness, tense and uncomfortable, hardly daring to breathe. Squinting through a crack between two of the boxes, they could make out a dim light approaching. A man came into view, carrying a swinging oil-lamp. His face was in the shadow, but they could just make out the uniform of a ship's officer. For one awful moment he seemed to be coming straight towards them and they cowered lower, but he was simply checking the cargo. Then the light shone on his face, and Turlough stifled a gasp. The man's eyes were set in a strange blank stare, as though he were in a trance. Hands moved blindly to test the cords holding the crates. Like an automaton, the figure turned and went back the way it had come. The hatch closed with a muffled thump in the distance and Turlough breathed again.

'What was the matter with him?' he hissed to the Doctor. 'Did you see his eyes?'

The Doctor nodded. 'Almost as if he were hypnotised.' Then he gave a sudden grin. 'At least he didn't see the TARDIS,' he said, getting to his feet. 'Come on.' And he moved purposefully towards the companion-ladder, a reluctant Turlough at his heels.

Tegan was getting restless. She had put the chess-pieces away and now there was nothing to do but wait. A flick of the scanner switch still showed total blackness outside, and the room seemed very empty. Firmly she turned back to the console telling herself that she must stay alert and ready for any message that might arrive. Behind her, at the bottom of the scanner screen, something moved. It was a pair of hands. Someone was climbing up outside. At almost the same moment the lights began to dim and brighten, dim and brighten in the White Guardian's signal. Tegan rushed to the lever, but she was reluctant to turn it to full immediately and the lights remained dim. The power was not enough.

'I daren't give you any more,' she said desperately.

' . . . More . . . more . . . more . . .' came the echo.

On the scanner screen the hands were now followed by a face: a white face, oddly distorted, the way faces are when pressed against glass. Tegan still did not see it, she was too busy manipulating the lever. She was giving more energy than she would have liked, and the room was getting even dimmer. A wisp of smoke trickled from inside the console.

'Please hurry!' Tegan found herself entreating. 'You're causing an overload.' But she might have been talking to herself.

The face at the scanner drew back a little and came

17

into focus. It was a good-looking face, a young man's, with firm cheek-bones, crisp fair hair, and oddly penetrating eyes which were fixed on the girl at the console.

Tegan was oblivious of them; oblivious, indeed, of everything but the shape which was beginning to materialise faintly in front of her. An elderly man, she thought, wearing a head-dress rather like a helmet, and a ceremonial-looking cloak. It was difficult to tell exactly what he looked like, for he flickered like a candle-flame in the wind.

'Are you the White Guardian?' she demanded. The figure mouthed silently, and Tegan completely lost her cool.

'The message!' she yelled. 'The message – Hurry up!'

She moved the lever higher still, and the White Guardian's voice suddenly broke through in mid-sentence.

'. . . must not win. Tell the Doctor. Winner takes all . . .'

'. . . all . . . all . . . all . .' came the echo as the figure grew fainter.

In the silence that followed, the muffled explosion from the depths of the console sounded like a volcano erupting. There was a shower of sparks, the tenuous shape disappeared, and every light but one went out. All that remained was a dim glow from an emergency working light, and from the scanner screen itself. It was then that Tegan saw the face looking in. For a moment she was completely bewildered.

'Who are you?' she called. 'Are you the White Guardian?'

There was no answer, simply a dazzled smile, as though the sight of her had caused whoever it was to lose the power of speech. The smile changed suddenly to a look of anguish as the viewer seemed to overbalance, and abruptly he disappeared from view.

'Oh no!' Tegan exclaimed. She had suddenly remembered something. The scanner camera was positioned in the flashing light on the roof of the TARDIS. The young man's face had seemed so close on the screen, that it must have been near the lens – he must have climbed up there. After falling from the height of the roof he might be hurt. Without a second thought, she grabbed the torch which the Doctor had been using for his repair work and hurriedly opened the main door onto the blackness which lay beyond.

2
The Race

The Doctor and Turlough emerged slowly and cautiously through the hatchway at the top of the companion-ladder, and found themselves in a dimly lit alleyway below decks. There was no sign of the man they had been following, and the passage seemed to end in a blank wall.

'Dead end?' asked Turlough, almost hoping that it would be. But the Doctor, running his hands over the surface in front of him, shook his head. The tips of his fingers had come in contact with a tell-tale crack.

'It's a door,' he said softly, pressing his ear to the wood and listening. 'Can't hear anything.' He looked at Turlough, an unspoken question in his eye. Turlough nodded, somewhat reluctantly. Taking a deep breath, the Doctor shoved the door open with his shoulder and they both walked through.

The room in which they found themselves was cramped and low-ceilinged and the air was full of tobacco smoke. A group of men were playing cards; another, lying on his bunk, was darning a sock; someone was idly picking at a banjo. There was no pause in the activity, but six pairs of eyes were turned to the newcomers.

The Doctor was the first to recover himself.

'How d'you do?' he said, with an affable smile all round. There was a vague murmur as a couple of them returned the greeting. The rest either nodded briefly or did not even bother to do that. The Doctor and Turlough might not have been there for all the notice that was taken of them. They exchanged a puzzled look. 'Who are they?' Turlough asked, under his breath. 'The crew,' answered the Doctor, in the same way. To Turlough's surprise and discomfiture, the Doctor suddenly strode forward to one of the bunks, and with a firm hand started testing the mattress.

'Not bad,' he said, in a loud bluff voice.

'Are you insane?' Turlough hissed, longing to drag him out of the room. 'What d'you think you're doing?'

'Behaving as though we've just joined the crew,' was the Doctor's soft answer. And then more loudly, 'This one'll do for me. You take the top.' And to Turlough's horror, he picked up a newspaper lying on the table, sat firmly on the bottom bunk, and calmly began reading. Turlough sat next to him. He could not think of anything else to do. Then he realised why the Doctor was holding the paper up in front of their faces. It made a perfect screen for them to confer behind.

'Where are we?' Turlough wanted to know. 'Planet Earth again?'

'It looks like it,' was the Doctor's answer. 'Edwardian England, judging by the uniform.' His eye was momentarily distracted by the headlines: *First British submarine launched,* he read. 'Yes – that would be about 1901, as far as I remember.'

Peering over the paper, Turlough realised that every man in the room, although pretending not to be interested, was in actual fact subjecting them to a covert examination. He found it unnerving.

'Why don't they say something?' he asked.

'Sizing us up.' The Doctor was unruffled. 'A fo'c's-

'le's pretty cramped. It's important to know what sort of men you're going to be sharing it with. After all, we could be cooped up here together for months. If we were here for the trip, that is,' he added, to Turlough's great relief. He thought he had never seen a rougher collection than these sailors, with their unshaven faces and watchful eyes.

'Shouldn't we be getting back to the TARDIS?' he suggested, trying not to sound too nervous. He was not reassured by the Doctor's next reply. They were to stay until they found out why the White Guardian had sent them here. Worse was to come. The Doctor was murmuring something in a serious voice, something about preserving the peace and harmony of the Universe.

'I hardly think that's at stake, is it?' Turlough whispered back, with what he hoped was squashing irony. But when he looked round the faces of the crew again, he was not at all sure. They might not threaten the entire universe, but they certainly looked as though they could threaten Turlough's particular bit of it, and that was all that mattered to him.

'Just as well we didn't bring Tegan with us,' the Doctor reflected. 'A woman below decks would have started a riot!'

A fo'c's'le may not be a suitable place for a woman, but a hold is not very comfortable either, particularly when it is dark and there are rats. 'And particularly when someone is following you,' Tegan thought to herself. There was no sign of the young man who had fallen from the roof of the TARDIS, although she had shone her torch in every direction. The trouble was that every time she stopped walking and listened, the floorboards creaked behind her as though someone else had not quite stopped in time. She reached the pile of crates as the Doctor and Turlough had done and was shining her torch along, when out of the corner of her eye she caught sight of writing on one of them. Hungry for information, she swung her torch onto it. The word *Striker* leapt out at her in its beam. That was no help! Behind her, somewhere, the floorboards squeaked again.

'Where are you?' Tegan called out, goaded. Silence. She walked to the end of the line of boxes and stopped. Behind her, like an echo, were someone else's footsteps. There was a clink of metal for a second. Quickly Tegan switched off her torch, slipped round the end of the crates and crouched behind one of them, holding her breath. Slithering, halting steps passed on the other side, paused, and then went on their way. Tegan stayed where she was, silent, crouched down in the gloom. There was a grating noise, and a dim shaft of light as the hatch was raised again. She could just make out feet disappearing up the ladder and then there was silence once more. Tegan waited another minute. Still nothing happened. With a sigh of relief, she switched on her torch, and was just about to get up when she caught sight of something that froze her to the spot. Next to her were a pair of feet in polished boots. Slowly she rose, shining her torch inch by inch up the figure standing there. The beam revealed well-pressed trousers, the brass button of an officer's jacket, a wing collar, and then came to rest on a slightly averted face. It was the young man she had seen in the scanner. He was completely immobile: almost like a tailor's dummy. Tegan was puzzled.

'Hello –' she quavered tentatively.

Immediately the officer took a quick step forward, trapping her with her back to the crates, and his face

24

came to life in a smile of great charm.

'Fascinating,' he said, with every appearance of sincerity. 'Who are you?'

'He's going to take me for a stowaway,' Tegan thought in despair. And sure enough, those were the young man's very next words.

'Yes. You're a stowaway. And I should put you in irons.'

But as his hands moved to grab her, Tegan ducked under his arm, dodged round to the other side of the crates and switched off her torch.

'Where are you?' came his voice.

Tegan did not reply. Slowly, hardly daring to breathe, she crept along the line of crates, peering every now and then through the spaces between them. She could see the ladder in the dim light from the companionway above. The hatch had been left open! She looked at it longingly. Should she make a dash for it, or should she try and get back to the TARDIS? 'The ladder,' Tegan thought. She dare not risk giving away the TARDIS's presence. Gingerly she rounded the end of the piled boxes and bumped straight into another immobile figure. Even as she recoiled, it turned its head, and, in the light from the companionway, she saw that it was another officer. It blinked into life and stretched its hands out towards her. But Tegan was ready. She side-stepped, swung the torch against the back of the man's head, and ran. When she reached the ladder, sobbing for breath, and looked back, there was no sign of the pursuit. The hold was dark and silent once more. Cautiously Tegan began to climb. Hardly daring to raise her head above the hatchway, she peered round. A dimly lit alleyway stretched to the left. Empty, she saw with relief. Carefully, she turned to see what lay to the right.

Immediately her eyes fell on a familiar pair of polished boots. Looking up, desparingly, she saw the young man from the scanner screen gazing down at her. He was still smiling. She was about to retreat, but a quick glance over her shoulder revealed the second officer now standing at the bottom of the ladder.

'Allow me,' said the smiling young man above, stretching out a hand to help her up. Tegan was terrified.

'It isn't possible!' she stuttered. 'How did you get up here? You were down there . . . I don't understand . . .'

He took not the slighest notice of what she was saying, but went on looking into her eyes with great concentration.

'Why are you afraid?' he asked in an interested voice. 'I'm not going to hurt you.'

Tegan was not at all sure about that, but as he had a firm grip of her arm, there was little she could do.

'I want to please you,' he said, with such convincing charm that Tegan almost relaxed. But not for long.

'Would you like me to find your friends for you?'

'What friends?' she stalled.

'The two you're looking for.'

Tegan struggled and kicked, now thoroughly alarmed. 'What have you done with them?' she wanted to know.

'Nothing. I haven't met them yet,' the young man replied, holding her in a firm but gentle grasp. 'I'll take you to them, if that's what you'd like.'

Tegan stopped fighting and looked at him.

'Yes. That's what I'd like,' she said.

At once he released her, and started to walk away down the companionway. Tegan stood looking after him, quite unable to make him out. He turned to make sure she was following.

'Please,' he smiled. And she found herself walking along at his side, almost companionably, while the soft voice went gently on. 'You won't try to run away again, will you? You see –' He broke off and stopped to look at her. 'I find you fascinating. Quite fascinating.' The remark was not intended as a compliment, she was sure, it was a simple statement of fact. As Tegan stared into his eyes she discovered that they were dark and deep. 'Like space,' she thought to herself, vaguely. And like space, they seemed limitless and empty.

A threatening shadow loomed over the newspaper, and the Doctor lowered it, to see one of the card-players standing in front of them. He was a big burly man, but his expression was good-humoured.

'The name's Jackson,' he said. 'Got your gear stowed?'

'Yes thanks.' The Doctor smiled pleasantly, and decided it was time they introduced themselves. 'This is Turlough. And I'm the Doctor.' The effect of these words was surprising. Jackson had been in the middle of nodding an acknowledgement to Turlough, but stopped dead and turned back immediately to the Time Lord.

'The Doctor! You are, are you!' he said.'And about time too.' And over his shoulder he called out, 'He's here, lads. The Doctor's aboard.'

'You've been expecting me?' There was relief in the Doctor's query.

'More than expecting you, Slush. We've been waiting for you,' Jackson replied.

The Doctor threw Turlough a delighted look. Now, at last, it seemed that they were going to find out more about their task. But Jackson's next words were not particularly enlightening.

'Where've you been, eh?' he enquired in a disgruntled way. 'We've had nothing but hard tack since we came aboard, haven't we lads?'

There was a chorus of agreement from the crew, and then several more comments.

'Proper food, that's what we want. None of your stinking greasy messes,' came from another of the card-players.

'Not like the last cook we sailed with,' and Jackson spat on the floor at the memory. The Doctor's face was a study.

'Of course' he muttered to himself. And then, as the men went back to their game, he said in a rather rueful aside to Turlough, 'Seaman's slang. The Doctor happens to be what they call the ship's cook.'

'And "Slush?" ' Turlough whispered back.

'Same thing. Different nickname,' replied the Doctor. But he was not cast down for long and very soon had managed to get himself introduced to the other card-players, Farley, Wade and Collier. It seemed that the newspaper was two days old, and had been brought aboard in someone's pocket. The men had been battened under hatches ever since. In fact, as he soon discovered, they had no memory of actually coming aboard at all. His first thought was that they must have celebrated their last night ashore a little too well. But it turned out that Jackson did not drink; he had signed the pledge and was a staunch teetotaller – and yet he remembered nothing either. The men did recall signing on, however, because they had done that when they were aboard, and, unusually, they had been paid a month's wages in advance. There was no complaint about the Captain's meanness.

'Stands to make a packet, I daresay, if we win,' was

Collier's comment.

'Win what?' Turlough wanted to know. They all turned to stare at him in surprise.

'The race, lad! The race!' Jackson looked at him pityingly, as though he were half-witted. Collier gave a knowing grin. 'Green hand, are you?' He was obviously about to enjoy himself at the newcomer's expense, and they all crowded round ready for a bit of sport. 'Why is it I always bring out the bully in people?' Turlough thought to himself sadly. But under the Doctor's watchful eye, the ribbing they gave him was not too bad. In fact it included some very good advice, for their stories about the horrors of going aloft contained a lot of practical information. He must never let go of the lifeline until his feet were on the deck, and he must keep his eyes open, and learn.

'Know why a pig can never be a sailor?' Collier leered into this ear. 'Cos it can't look aloft.' He dug Turlough hard in the ribs and they all laughed uproariously at this witticism. But the guffaws died into an uneasy silence as one of the officers walked in. He stood impassively, then pointed to the Doctor and beckoned. 'Looks like you're wanted.' Jackson said quietly. The Doctor rose to his feet. There was still no word from the officer, just a peremptory nod, and he turned on his heel and left, clearly expecting the Doctor to follow him. Turlough was going to get up too, but quietly and firmly the Doctor pressed him back into his seat. 'You know where the TARDIS is, if things get difficult,' he said softly as he passed.

The officer's arrival seemed to have put a damper on the crew's spirits, for there was no more laughter or leg-pulling. Turlough was not particularly happy, either. Even though the Doctor frequently irritated him, he missed his company. There was something

29

very reassuring about it.

'Where've they taken him?' he asked.

'Poop quarters,' came from a surly Collier.

'First Mate wanted to see him, I daresay,' Jackson added, and then, with a touch of sourness, 'Living like lords they are, back there. Every luxury.'

'While we make do with salt junk and hard tack,' Collier added his grumble.

To his annoyance, Turlough found his concern for the Doctor growing. His basic philosophy learnt from life so far was to look after himself first and not to fall into the trap of caring too much about anybody else. But he found himself saying, in a slightly anxious voice, 'He'll be all right, won't he?'

Jackson's reply was not encouraging. 'Who can tell?' he said fatalistically, and shrugged his shoulders.

3
Here She Blows!

The room into which the Doctor was shown was in
marked contrast to the fo'c's'le. It had panelled walls
and a polished floor; a long gleaming table ran down
the centre of it, lit by candles, and laid formally for a
meal. There was champagne on ice and there were tall
fluted glasses. The officer nodded towards the wine
and then withdrew. The Doctor took this as an
invitation to help himself and was just debating
whether or not he should, when out of the shadows
stepped Tegan. Ignoring the Doctor's startled exclamation, she burst into a frantic explanation of how
the console had blown up and how she had seen the
face on the scanner, how the White Guardian had
failed to materialise fully and how his message had not
made sense.

'"Winner takes all",' she quoted in scorn. 'What
does that mean?'

'We are on a racing yacht,' the Doctor observed
thoughtfully. Tegan was startled. 'How d'you know?'

'We've been talking to the crew,' he explained.

'Well I hope they're not as peculiar as the officers,'
was her rejoinder. 'The one I've met is very strange.'

The door opened almost before she finished speaking, and they swung round, ready for anything. What
they saw could have been a tableau from a waxworks.
Three men stood there. The foremost was a tall

distinguished figure, with a dark saturnine face, and a uniform covered in gold braid. Like the two officers at his heels, he stood motionless and expressionless for a second, then suddenly clicked into action and stepped forward with a courtly bow.

'Welcome aboard. Delighted you could join us.' His voice was smooth and reassuring, but there was an air of command about him, and a great reserve behind his easy authority. 'Captain Striker, at your service.'

'How d'you do,' the Doctor began. I'm –'

'– the Doctor –' Striker interrupted smoothly, as though he knew all about them. 'And Miss Tegan, I believe. Allow me to present my officers.' Silently, the two officers saluted.

'They're a funny lot,' Jackson said.

'The after guard always are.' Collier was as cynical as usual, but Turlough hardly heard him.

'What d'you mean "funny"?' he asked.

The men were not very articulate, but he gathered that few of them had set eyes on the Captain, and that the bosun got most of his orders from the First Mate.

'Did he say where the ship was going?' Turlough asked keenly.

They shuffled uneasily. 'Don't remember,' someone muttered. Eyes slid away from his shiftily. They obviously did not want to discuss it.

'We're here for the race. That's all that matters.' But if Jackson thought he had changed the subject, he reckoned without their questioner. Turlough had decided to impress the Doctor by finding out as much as he could.

'Where are we racing *to?*' he repeated. 'Where's the finish?'

There was a sudden grinding jolt, and Jackson

looked up. The oil lamps hanging from the ceiling were swaying from side to side, and from the distance came the sound of the bosun's pipe. Immediately the men's dazed expressions vanished and all was confidence and action again.

'Here she blows,' Jackson said. 'This is what we've been waiting for. The wind.'

In the stateroom the wine in the glasses swished from side to side. One fell over, and a dark red stain spread over the linen. The Doctor put out a hand to steady his claret, and caught Tegan's eye. She looked distinctly queasy.

'I hope it's not going to be too rough,' she muttered. 'I'm not a very good sailor.'

Striker and his officers appeared oblivious of the movement of the ship. They sat, staring blankly ahead, eating and drinking in silence, their faces as impassive as they had been since the beginning of the meal. The shrill squealing of the bosun's pipe sounded from somewhere, and Tegan felt her stomach beginning to heave up and down with the boat.

'Brave heart, Tegan!' came the Doctor's encouraging whisper across the table, but all she could manage was a watery smile.

'It's not my heart I'm worried about,' she whispered back.

The door was flung open and a voice she recognised spoke.

'Breaking out the rum ration, sir.'

It was her friend of the scanner screen who stood there, his face elated and energy vibrating in his movements. The effect of his arrival on Striker and the other two officers was electric, as though they had come to life.

33

'Good,' Striker's tone was incisive, his introductions perfunctory. 'My First Mate, Mr Marriner, – I believe you've met.' Marriner's salute and short-lived smile in her direction showed that even he now had other things on his mind.

'Everything in order?' the Captain was asking him. 'Are the crew ready?'

'Being prepared,' came the enigmatic reply. The ship shuddered violently. Striker and the two officers sprang to their feet, leaving the Doctor and Tegan sitting in bewilderment.

'I must apologise,' broke in Striker, courteous as always, 'for this rather abrupt end to dinner.'

As the Doctor and Tegan pushed back their chairs to get up, the ship lurched more violently still. There was a crash from the table as several more glasses fell, and they were both thrown back into their seats.

'Look to the lady, Mr Marriner,' was the Captain's brisk command, and he hurried from the room, his officers behind him.

Marriner was clearly delighted to offer Tegan his arm, but she pulled back, demanding to know where they were going. 'To the wheel-house,' he answered, and before she could raise another objection she was whisked through the doorway. By the time the Doctor had struggled up from his chair there was no sign of her. There was no sign of her in the companionway, either, and he looked from left to right, trying to decide which way to go.

Turlough was equally lost. At the sound of the bosun's pipe everyone in the fo'c's'le had appeared to go berserk. There was a mad rush of men for the doorway, and he was jostled from side to side. Grasping Collier's arm as he passed he asked what was

34

going on. 'Grog ration,' was the brief explanation and then he was alone in the empty fo'c's'le, looking at the half-darned sock, the cards lying higgledy-piggledy on the floor, and the deserted banjo. A second later Jackson was back.

'Come on, lad,' he shouted, shoving Turlough ahead of him. It was not until they were half way along the passageway that Turlough discovered to his horror that they were about to go up aloft, and by then it was too late to turn back.

The Doctor was still looking for the wheel-house when he heard the sound of running feet. He flattened himself against the bulkhead as several sailors dashed past him one after the other and shinned up the companion-ladder to the deck above. Two more arrived at the double, and as the first bent to retie a shoe-lace he saw that it was Turlough. The man behind overtook him and disappeared up the ladder, with a shout of 'Come on, lad.' If Turlough heard, he certainly made no move, other than to straighten up with a satisfied expression. There was a murmur 'Not going with them?' in his ear, which made him jump, and when he spun round he saw the Doctor smiling at him with complete understanding.

'Going aloft? The rigging's no place for a coward like me!' Turlough grinned back. It was rather a relief that the Doctor knew him so well, at least he did not have to pretend. And it was not too difficult to confess that he had failed to find anything out about the race, except for the fact that the crew apparently knew very little about it either: information which interested the Doctor, but did not seem to surprise him.

'Can't we get back to the TARDIS?' Turlough asked, looking round nervously.

'Not till we've found Tegan,' the Doctor answered.

But before either of them could move a step, their skin prickled to the sound of a blood-curdling scream. Somewhere there was a man in mortal terror.

The same cry halted Tegan. She had just been helped up from a companionway by Marriner, and she stopped dead, tense and alarmed.

'What was that?' she gasped. Marriner's expression never changed, and his tone was as calm and pleasant as usual.

'One of the crew going aloft. It sometimes affects them that way, especially when it's the first time.'

Tegan was horrified. 'The first time! You mean you're sending a completely inexperienced crewman aloft? In a race!'

'They soon get used to it,' Marriner smiled at her. He moved on quite unperturbed, but Tegan was not to be put off.

'Now wait a minute –' she said, as she caught up with him. She meant business, by the sound of her voice, but it died away in disbelief as she caught sight of something in the corridor ahead.

'Wet suits!' she exclaimed, rushing forward to examine them. There they were, hanging in a row on pegs, with shelves of other equipment below. 'What are wet suits doing on an Edwardian sailing-ship?'

Without a word Marriner took her by the arm and hustled her along the passageway to a door at the end, flung it open and hurried her through into what was clearly the wheel-house. The whole place seemed to be glassed in, and to Tegan's surprise it was pitch dark outside. Somehow she had expected a race to start in daylight. But before she had time to comment, or to do more than glance at the polished brass of the nautical instruments round the walls, there came a curt com-

36

mand from the far end of the room.

'Mr Mate.' It was Striker, standing by the helms-man at the wheel. Excusing himself briefly, Marriner hurried to the Captain's side.

'Are you all right?' she heard the Doctor's anxious voice asking. He and Turlough had just hurried in and were looking very relieved to see her. Tegan rushed across to them, her words tumbling over each other.

'You'll never guess what I've seen! Wet suits! In one of the companionways! Underwater gear – like scuba-divers wear!'

'On an Edwardian ship!' Turlough was scathing. But there was something about Tegan's certainty that was convincing.

'Wait a minute,' said the Doctor. 'This might tell us where we are.' He had caught sight of a chart spread out on one of the tables. Tegan and Turlough hurried over to join him and in a second the three of them were poring over it.

Turlough was the first to give up.

'It doesn't make sense!' he said in disgust.

But Tegan had a feeling she was on the right track. 'It's to do with the race, I'm sure,' she said. 'Marker buoys! It shows the positions of the marker buoys!'

'Marker buoys?' They're considerably more than that –'

The gravity in the Doctor's voice startled them. But before he could explain, Striker was calling out au-thoritatively, 'Mr Mate – we'll look at our competi-tors, please.'

Marriner pressed a brass lever and the polished wooden top of a fitment opened, to reveal a bank of switches. A touch on one of them produced a gentle humming noise and a large panel in the wall slid slowly upwards.

'Electronics!' exclaimed Tegan, her mouth dropping open. 'What date *is* this ship?'

She and Turlough stared at each other in bewilderment, but the Doctor only had eyes for what the panel revealed. It was a huge screen, like a gigantic scanner.

'Look!' he said urgently.

It was not sea which surrounded them; there were no waves, no long swell, no distant horizon; there was nothing but a vast blackness, spangled with far-away stars.

'We're in space,' the Doctor said.

Into view glided a square-rigged eighteenth-century frigate, so close they felt they could almost have touched her. Beyond were the tall lines of a clipper; beyond her, a galleon; beyond, a shape that was older still, a hint of the Phoenician in her prow; another and another, floating in the dark as far as the eye could see.

'What are they?' Tegan whispered.

'Space ships,' answered the Doctor.

4
Marker Buoy

The Doctor seemed unaware of Turlough's presence at his elbow; he was completely engrossed, taking in every detail of the strange ships on the screen.

'Fascinating,' he said. 'The technology is amazing.'

'Why waste it on *that* though?' Turlough was incredulous. 'What are they trying to achieve? Is it some sort of game? It's not real!'

'The crew are real enough,' observed the Doctor. Turlough thought of Jackson, Collier and the rest, with their earthy humour and their mild bullying, and he had to agree. Definitely human. He was not so sure about the officers. His eyes went to the Captain, frozen motionless again in his position by the helmsman, then to Marriner, still and silent at the computer, and he had a sudden inspiration. 'Androids?' he asked. But the Doctor shook his head slowly. 'Much more complicated.'

They were interrupted by a low groan from Tegan. She was leaning against the wall, looking distinctly green. 'I feel terrible,' she moaned. Marriner was at her side almost before she had finished speaking, offering his arm and asking to be allowed to escort her to her cabin.

'You'll have to hurry,' was the faint response. 'I'm going to be very sick.'

And before the Doctor could prevent it she had left

the wheel-house with the First Mate. He tried to follow them, but an officer barred the way and Turlough put out a restraining hand. The last thing he wanted was for the Doctor to start throwing his weight about. It could only lead to trouble.

'Tegan will be all right,' he said soothingly. 'Whatever's going on here, nobody has *threatened* us.'

'*Yet,*' answered the Doctor, cryptically.

Marriner half-led, half-carried Tegan along several deserted passageways. Her seasickness was now so acute that she hardly noticed which way they were going. She clung to Marriner's arm as though it were a lifeline. The cabin he showed her into was simply a blur as far as she was concerned, and she collapsed onto the bed. 'I just want to die,' she groaned, and then became conscious of a glass of something being held out to her. From what seemed a long way off she heard a voice saying 'Drink this', and she was just about to take it when a warning bell sounded somewhere in her mind. With an enormous effort, gripping the edge of the bed as hard as she could, she pulled herself together. Marriner's face swam into view again, and his hand, still holding the glass of liquid.

'What is it?' she asked suspiciously.

Marriner smiled. 'A mixture.'

She took the glass and sniffed warily at the contents.

'Rum?' she asked. Marriner did not reply, simply smiled soothingly, and said again, 'Drink it.'

Tegan put the glass down firmly on the bedside table. 'No thanks.'

Marriner shook his head in amusement. 'It'll make you feel better,' he explained.

'Drink it yourself, then,' was Tegan's tart rejoinder. 'You need it more than I do.'

Marriner ignored her comments, but he clearly understood her suspicions.

'It's quite safe,' he said. And when this failed to reassure her, he took the glass from the table, raised it to her in a silent toast, drank from it himself and then held it out to her once more. Slowly Tegan took it and raised it to her lips. She had just decided that the only thing she could possibly keep down was something as innocuous as water, when to her surprise that was what it turned out to be. Cool, clear spring water. Or rather, that was what it tasted like. Limpid and refreshing, it slid down her throat, and the giddiness in her head slipped away and the tension in her stomach relaxed and she felt as though she were floating. Dreamily she lay back on the bunk. She was just conscious of the coverlet being pulled gently over her and through a haze she heard Marriner's voice. 'I must return to duty. The first marker buoy will be coming up soon.'

'Marker buoy –' Tegan's speech sounded slurred. Her eyes closed drowsily and she lost consciousness.

Venus glimmered, distant, but clearly visible through the forrard port of the wheel-house. Striker stirred, as though he had just woken from sleep, but when he spoke his voice was measured and precise. 'Check our exact position.' An officer crossed immediately to one of the computer terminals and Striker continued, with some satisfaction, 'Gentlemen, we are about to round our first planet.'

'Planet?' Turlough was startled. He thought for a minute he could not have heard correctly, but the Doctor did not appear at all surprised.

'Remember the chart?' he said in a low voice.

'The one Tegan insisted was plotting the marker

buoys?' Turlough replied.

'Yes' the Doctor said. 'She was right. If you'd looked more carefully you'd have recognised the pattern. It's a map of the solar system containing Earth. The marker buoys are the planets.'

Turlough did not take this in for a second. The idea of using planets to mark a race course seemed so extraordinary. But before he could ask any questions the Doctor was speaking in a low urgent voice in his ear, 'Find out where Marriner's taken Tegan. Now! Slip out while nobody's looking.'

Turlough glanced round. The Doctor was right. They were unobserved. All eyes were on the distant planet ahead.

'There's no need to whisper, Doctor,' came Striker's voice suddenly from the far end of the wheel-house. 'You and your companions are free to come and go as you wish. You are guests, not prisoners.'

Turlough could not resist a momentary smile of pleasure at the Doctor's discomfiture. Then he did as he had been told.

The moment the door closed behind him, the Doctor went into action. It was vital to find out more about this strange race as quickly as possible, and he had decided that the best person to tell him was the Captain. Idly, as though drawn by the mysterious charm of the planet, he sauntered over to the porthole and stared out.

'Very aptly named,' he commented. 'After the goddess of beauty herself.'

Striker, standing by the helmsman, turned blank eyes in his direction.

'Venus,' the Doctor added softly, as though he had been asked a question.

'Ah yes. Venus.' Striker came to life. 'Our first

obstacle. Our next major obstacle is the Greek.'

He operated a switch, and the line of sailing-ships came once more into view on the screen. Almost as if it were alive, the scanner picked out one in particular and homed in. The banked oars of a great Greek galley came into close-up, its sail bellied out, and then, closer still, the scanner moved in on its captain, seated on a lavish throne and studying a chart.

'Critas the Greek,' came Striker's precise voice. 'The only captain who could possibly beat me.'

The Doctor was so intrigued that for a moment he forgot the object of the exercise. His gaze had dwelt lovingly on the eye painted on the galley's bow, on the dolphin's tail of the stern, and on the linen chiton of the man sitting there . . . He pulled himself abruptly together.

'The period detail of your ships is impressively accurate,' he said, echoing the slightly pedantic tones of the Captain.

'There is no point in the race otherwise,' Striker replied.

'Accurate except for one thing.' the Doctor's voice was soft, but he made quite sure that it was audible. And it was not until he knew that he had Striker's attention that he spoke again. 'The jewel' he said. And immediately, almost as though reading his thoughts, the scanner moved in close on a ring on the Greek's finger.

'That isn't contemporary, is it?' he asked, with deceptive innocence, as they both stared at the great cabuchon ruby. 'Seventeenth-century Spanish, surely.'

Striker looked at him sharply, then back at the screen.

"You're very observant,' he said.

'The only thing out of period. I wonder why?' The Doctor's mild comment seemed to hang in the air for a second, and then, recovering quickly from his discomfiture, Striker switched the scanner back to a view of Venus, now closer still.

'When you meet Critas, you must ask him,' he said smoothly, and turned his back.

Turlough had completely lost his way in the maze of passages below decks and was beginning to think he would never find Tegan's cabin. To his relief, he heard a hatch grate open and a figure began descending the companion-ladder ahead. He hurried forward to ask for directions, and for a brief second the notes of a sea-shanty drifted down. Somewhere overhead the crew were singing. Then the hatch was banged down again and the music was cut off. When he reached the foot of the ladder, he discovered it was not a member of the crew who stood there, but one of the officers. There was something about the motionless figure that would have marked it out even without the uniform. But as Turlough peered into the frozen face, the eyes moved suddenly and looked back at him. Momentarily disconcerted, he did not know what to say. Then, pulling himself together, and with a jerk of his head towards the ladder, he asked, 'Where does this lead?' 'The deck,' came the brief reply, and Turlough felt all sense of reality beginning to leave him. The ship was moving through space, and yet he could have sworn he had heard men singing above.

As if in confirmation the officer went on, 'The crew are busy up there.' 'Doing what?' Turlough asked.

'Hauling on the halyards.'

That was the final straw. 'Halyards!' he burst out. 'On a space ship?'

44

'Certainly,' came the imperturbable reply. 'We observe the spirit as well as the rules of the race.'

Turlough shook his head in disbelief. It was clear that he was not going to get any sense out of this creature, and he turned to continue his search. But before he had taken three steps down the passageway, a voice called after him, 'The lady's cabin is on the starboard side.' The 'thank you' he was about to say suddenly froze in his throat. How had the man known he was looking for Tegan? An idea began to surface in his mind but he suppressed it. Clearly it had been a case of putting two and two together. The man had simply guessed. Nevertheless, he hurried down the passage, almost at a run, very glad to get away.

Tegan drifted up from the warmth of sleep to feel someone shaking her arm. For a moment she was reluctant to open her eyes, but when she did she found Turlough looking down at her. 'Are you all right?' he asked.

'Of course!' she answered.

'Are you sure?'

Tegan had never felt better in her life. 'I feel marvellous.' She stretched luxuriously, for the moment not remembering where she was. 'Not space-sick any more?' She sat up with a jerk. Turlough was examining the glass she had drunk from. He sniffed at it. 'Probably the same stuff that they give to the crew,' he said, putting it back on the table. 'It doesn't seem to do them any harm.' 'I'm pleased to hear it,' Tegan said dryly, and swinging her legs over, she sat up and looked round the room properly for the first time. What she saw gave her a shock. It was not the disorder of the things lying around that startled her, but the actual objects themselves. There, hanging on a

45

hatstand, was the fancy dress frock she had been lent by Lady Cranleigh. And there, tossed idly onto a chair, was a tennis racket she recognised. She could see her name burnt into the handle. And the broken string. It was the one she had used at school, when she was fourteen. The dressing-table looked familiar, too. And the chair in the corner . . . She could feel her heart beginning to thump uncomfortably, and breathlessly she looked at Turlough. He obviously felt the same.

'Some of it's – quite familiar, isn't it?' he said, in an odd voice, glancing round.

'It's a sort of weird mix of – my room on the TARDIS and my bedroom in Brisbane.' Curiously Tegan picked up a small silver frame and her voice rose in a squeak as she saw the photograph it contained. 'Aunt Vanessa!' It was indeed her favourite aunt, smiling fondly back at her from the picture as she used to in life. 'I don't believe it!' Tegan looked wildly round the room and recognised more and more.

'It's – as though someone's been rummaging around in my memories.'

'Maybe they have.' Turlough's voice was strained. 'I'm beginning to find this ship very strange.' He grabbed Tegan's arm. 'Come on,' he said urgently. 'Let's get back to the Doctor!'

Venus was nearer still, and the churning belt of clouds surrounding her was getting ominously close. All eyes in the wheel-house were fixed ahead. Striker's attention was so concentrated that he answered the Doctor's questions almost absently. Perhaps, indeed, he would not otherwise have answered them at all, the Doctor thought; so he pressed on while he had the opportunity.

46

'Why are you doing this?'

'The race?' Striker murmured in an abstracted voice. 'As a diversion.'

The Doctor felt his anger rising, but with great control kept his voice as even as possible. 'And the crews for the ships . . . You've collected them from their different time zones. Just as a diversion, too?'

Striker did not reply for a minute. He sounded bored. 'They are Ephemerals.'

'Ephemerals?' the Doctor queried.

Striker's contempt was clear. 'Beings like yourself,' he said.

The Doctor could contain himself no longer. 'You had no right to do it!' he burst out. 'Those crews are human beings! They're real! Living, breathing flesh and blood!'

His fury had not the slightest effect on Striker, who simply turned away, indifferent. For a second. Then he swung round, his face alive and intent, and interested.

'Wait! You are a time-dweller – no –' It was almost as though he could hear the Doctor mentally correcting him. 'You travel in time – a Time Lord –'

'You can read my thoughts!' It came to the Doctor in a flash and he wondered why he had not tumbled to it before, it explained so many things. But the Captain was continuing, disdainfully, 'A Lord of Time! Are there lords in such a small domain?'

'Small? Where do you function?' the Doctor asked. Striker turned cold distant eyes on him. 'The endless wastes of Eternity.'

For a second the Doctor's heart seemed to freeze under that icy stare, and then all was bustle and confusion, and a voice was shouting urgently, 'Marker buoy, sir! Marker buoy!'

They turned.

Venus now filled the entire port, or rather a portion of the planet did, growing larger and larger and closer and closer every second. They seemed about to hurl themselves into the sulphurous fog around her.

'Marker buoy!' The shout was more frantic still. 'Coming up on the starboard bow!'

5
One Down!

The same excitement caught Tegan and Turlough as they hurried back along the companionways to the wheel-house. The bosun's pipe started shrilling urgently, and there was the noise of running feet and shouting. Then, as they rounded a corner, they came upon a surprising scene. A queue of men, wearing what looked like wet suits, was moving towards one of the companion-ladders. At the foot of it sat an officer, doling out 'rum' from a large cask. As each man in turn took his tot, he downed it in one, slammed the jigger back onto the cask, lowered a transparent cover over his face, and was then shoved on his way up by another officer. Even as they arrived, a scuffle broke out. A man had reached the foot of the ladder and jibbed, struggling and refusing to climb. It was Jackson. And it took the combined efforts of Collier and the officer to get him up.

'Of course,' Turlough said softly, almost to himself. 'He doesn't drink, – he hasn't had his tot.'

'What's that got to do with it?' Tegan asked.

'They'd never get them up there without it!'

'Up where?' Tegan still did not understand.

'Up into the rigging,' Turlough said, impatiently.

Tegan was completely taken aback. 'The rigging!' she exclaimed. 'In space! It's mad! This ship can't function like a real sailing-ship!'

'Never heard of the solar wind?' Turlough asked. 'Ten protons per centimetre moving outward from the sun at 440 miles a second. That's a supersonic velocity, and if it can deflect the tails of comets, it can move us as well!'

'Take in the top gallant.'

Striker stood by the helmsman, totally in command. Marriner, relaying his orders, shouted down the speaking-tube.

'Get them aloft, bosun. Take in the top gallant.'

'A point-and-a-half to starboard, helmsman.' The sailor obeyed but the look he gave his Captain was one of pure terror. The Doctor sympathised.

'What are you doing?' he asked urgently. Striker ignored him.

'Hold her on course,' he said again. 'We'll cut it as fine as we can.'

'D'you think that's wise?' the Doctor asked tightly. Marriner seemed to share his concern.

'We're coming in too fast,' he called.

'Take in the upper topsail.' The Captain's order was relayed down the speaking-tube, 'Take in the upper topsail.'

'Come about or you'll crash!' the Doctor implored desperately.

'Certainly not. Hold her steady, helmsman.' The Captain was adamant, and seeing the wretched sailor struggling, the Doctor rushed to help him hold the wheel.

'Get them up there,' Marriner's shouts came thick and fast. 'Stand by to lower the gaffs. Get those men aloft –'

The black smog banks seemed to be rushing towards them at enormous speed, lightning flashing within them, and the helmsman gasped in horror.

'Hold her on course, man,' Striker grated, and then, with an impatient gesture, shoved the wretched sailor to one side and took his place at the wheel with the Doctor.

'What are we down to, Mr Mate?'

'Staysail, fore lower topsail and main trysail,' came the reply. 'If we strip her any more she won't steer.'

'Heave to!' demanded the Doctor.

'And lose our chance of being first round? Never!' There was elation in Striker's voice and his face was transformed. 'This is the sort of excitement that makes eternity bearable.'

It was at that moment that Tegan and Turlough burst in – and cowered back in horror at the sight which filled the port – the shimmering heat of hell itself.

'What's happening?' Tegan cried.   'Stop!'

'We can't! We're running before the wind,' the Doctor called back. 'Some sort of ion drive.'

'We're going to hit!' Turlough shouted.

The ship lurched wildly. Everyone but the Doctor and Striker was thrown across the room. There was a momentary glimpse of clinging wisps of fog at the portholes, as though it was trying to suck them down – down into the sulphurous clouds, down to where acid fell like rain, to where the great wind whirled unceasingly, to the surface of the planet itself, molten with heat. Then they pulled away. The ship resumed even keel. Venus receded to the left of the screen. Slowly everyone began to pick themselves up, and there was the sound of distant cheering from the men aloft. Tegan could hardly believe her eyes when she saw Marriner's grin.

'A close shave, Captain,' he said.

'They'll never catch us now!' Striker was triumphant.

Turlough found he was shivering, whether with relief or fear he was not sure. 'We must have entered the gravitational pull of the planet,' he whispered to the Doctor. 'Why didn't we crash?'

'Luck,' came the sardonic reply. But Tegan heard it.

'Luck!' She was hopping mad and her fury was turned on Marriner and Striker. 'We could have been killed!' Her accusing look meant nothing to them. 'Worth risking to win,' Marriner answered mildly; Striker seemed to be communing with himself. 'We are determined to win.'

'And "winner takes all",' said the Doctor quietly.

'Let's see who's next to round her, Mr Marriner.' Striker operated the scanner screen, and into view, rounding the rim of Venus, sailed a galleon and a Greek battle cruiser.

'Critas and the *Buccaneer!*' came Marriner's excited comment. 'Neck and neck!'

Tegan looked at his face, and then at Striker's – animated and alive, the frozen look banished completely. But before she had time to draw the Doctor's attention to the transformation, a sudden blinding flash suffused the screen, and they reeled as shock waves hit the ship. On the scanner the Greek ship showed as nothing but a mass of flames. A second later there was another shattering explosion, and she disintegrated and disappeared completely. Where she had been was simply the blackness of space.

'Gravitational pull, would you say?' Nothing but detached interest was apparent in Striker's voice. Marriner was equally casual. 'Must have cut it a bit too fine. Bad luck, really.'

'Bad luck!' Tegan was on him like a tornado. 'Is

52

that all you can say! A ship has just been destroyed! Its entire crew wiped out!'

She might not have spoken for all the effect it had. Indeed Striker sounded positively cheerful as he glanced round the assembled company.

'We have a clear lead, gentlemen. And I intend to keep it. Mr Marriner, issue the crew an extra ration of rum. With the Captain's compliments.'

Marriner saluted and left the room, and Striker turned on his heel and went back to join the helmsman. Turlough was left looking at the Doctor.

'I've never seen a ship break up like that before,' he said. 'Was it gravitational pull?'

The Doctor shook his head. 'Unlikely. You saw how this was manoeuvred around Venus. Their ships can withstand enormous stress.'

Tegan still seemed dazed. 'Was it – sabotage?' she asked in a whisper.

'Or was it shot down?'

The Doctor's voice was grave. 'This race is getting serious. Someone is prepared to kill in order to win.'

'Win what?' Tegan felt completely bewildered. 'We don't even know what the prize is.'

'We must find out,' the Doctor replied. 'I think it's time we had a conference.'

Tegan glanced at Striker's broad shoulders, as he stood, with back towards them, by the wheel. With a sinking heart and a slight pang, she thought of Marriner.

'You don't think – *they* were responsible, do you?' she said. 'They can't be – murderers!'

To her surprise, instead of answering reassuringly, the Doctor turned her sharply to face the exit.

'Not here, Tegan. Your cabin,' he said, and pushed her and Turlough firmly into the corridor.

6
The Officers

Tegan stared blankly at the door which had just been shut in her face. 'What was all that about?' she asked in an aggrieved voice.

'Have you forgotten your room?' Turlough reminded her. 'All the things in it, – taken from your memory? These creatures must be able to mind read, we've got to be careful.'

At that moment one of the 'creatures' appeared. Round the corner of the passage way came Marriner. His smile was as charming as ever, his manner as courteous and urbane as he offered to escort Tegan to her cabin.

'I can find my own room, thanks,' was her snappy rejoinder, and she turned on her heel and walked away. The rebuff did not seem to put the First Mate off in the least, and he followed her quite happily.

Turlough watched them go, then quietly moved off in the opposite direction. He had a particular reason for wanting to be on his own.

In the wheel-house the Captain still stared blankly into space. The Doctor thought of Tegan's momentary suspicion. He too found it difficult to believe that their hosts were cold-blooded killers.

'Your assumptions are correct.' Striker suddenly spoke, without either turning round or looking at him.

'No one on this ship was responsible for the destruction of the Greek.'

'Who was, then?' the Doctor asked softly. 'Who did it?'

'I don't know.' Striker still stared into space. 'Sabotage is not against the rules of the race. It is simply less diverting.'

'It spoils the fun, you mean,' the Doctor said grimly. 'What *is* against the rules, then?'

Striker turned and looked at him. 'To go beyond.'

The Doctor was mystified.

'Beyond those limits we have chosen for ourselves,' he continued.

'You chose this type of ship,' the Doctor said, trying to work it out. 'And the crew –'

'– was selected from the relevant period of Earth history,' Striker finished the sentence for him.

'Why, though?' the Doctor went on. 'You didn't select them just to sail the ship. There's something else you need them for.'

The Captain looked at him coldly. 'Ephemerals offer a certain diversion,' he said, his manner returning to its usual reserve.

'The crudity of their minds amuses you!' The Doctor could feel anger beginning to well up in him again. 'Their primitive emotions!'

'Simply put, but in essence true,' and Striker turned away disdainfully.

'You talk as though they were toys!' the Doctor exploded.

Striker was unruffled. 'To me, they are,' he replied with lofty scorn.

The Doctor's voice was suddenly incisive. 'Then why is one of you taking this race so seriously?'

Striker stopped dead. And taking advantage of this

56

apparent uncertainty, the Doctor made for the door. There was a sharp 'Where are you going?', as Striker recovered, but the Doctor had made a discovery. For a brief second, Striker had not been able to read his mind. It was possible to distract these beings, to break their concentration, however briefly.

'Don't you *know* where I'm going?' he asked. The pause before Striker replied was barely noticeable.

'To Miss Tegan's cabin,' he answered.

'You didn't know, though, did you? Just for a second.' There was definite satisfaction in the Doctor's voice, and he left the wheel-house quite jauntily.

'Go away! Stop following me!' Tegan rounded on Marriner and almost spat the words at him. He had walked two paces behind her all the way from the wheel-house, and now that her cabin door was in sight she had felt brave enough to speak her mind.

'Why are you angry with me?' He sounded quite aggrieved, which annoyed her even more.

'Angry? I'm not angry, I'm disgusted! A ship blows up – everyone aboard is lost – and you don't even care!'

She had meant to sweep into her cabin with these final words, but Marriner forestalled her. With a quick step he moved in front of her and barred the way.

'You don't understand,' he said, as though talking to a child. 'They were not "lost", they merely transferred. Home.'

For a moment relief flooded through her. Everyone aboard that ship had been saved! But then she caught sight of Marriner's expression.

'You don't mean the *crew* were saved, do you?' She really could have hit him. 'You mean the officers!

Things like you! What happened to the crew? Were they all killed?'

'Ephemerals have such short lives in any case,' Marriner objected mildly. But Tegan was beside herself. 'Human beings, you mean,' she yelled at him.

'Whatever you wish to call them,' he answered with infuriating reasonableness. 'And on this ship, at least, they are treated well.'

'Well!' Tegan's voice was scathing. 'I happen to think human lives are just as valuable as yours.' And with a sweeping gesture she brushed him aside and went into her cabin. She could not resist sticking her head out again almost immediately, though. 'I happen to *be* a human being!' she said, her eyes flashing. Marriner obviously found her more irresistible than ever.

'You are different,' he said, dotingly. 'You are not like any Ephemeral I have ever met before.'

Before he could speak again the door was slammed in his face.

Turlough was alone. At last he had found a deserted companionway. Slowly and almost reluctantly he took the Cube from his pocket. The time had come to call on the Black Guardian. Turlough now hated his master almost as much as he feared him, but he knew that he must have assistance in order to survive, and as his own survival was Turlough's major concern, he managed to shut his eyes for the time being to the act which he knew the Black Guardian demanded of him in return.

'Can you hear me?' he whispered into the Communication Cube. And then more urgently, 'I need your help!'

Nothing happened. Turlough realised why a second

later. A seaman clattered down a ladder from the deck above. And then another, and another. As each one reached the bottom, he pushed back his space mask, his face hot and sweaty, but elated. Obviously excitement and the strange 'rum' mixture were a heady combination.

Turlough moved away. He rounded a corner into another alleyway, a darker one, with no companion-ladder in sight – and then he tried again.

'You must answer! I need your help!' he said, slightly desperately, into the Cube. 'What's going on here?'

The voice that sounded behind him was as chilling as ice. 'You are worthless to me.' He spun round to the tall looming figure of the Black Guardian himself. 'I have watched your progress,' the voice continued, and then a long arm was stretched towards him, the brocade of the sleeve glinting in the gloom of the corridor. Turlough stood mesmerised, like a rabbit trapped by a stoat. The Black Guardian's bony tapering fingers wrapped round his throat, and then it was too late, for struggle as he might, nothing could dislodge their grip. 'You have had many opportunities to destroy the Doctor.' There was no sense of effort in his captor's voice, although Turlough was now beginning to choke. 'I can't kill him,' he managed to gasp out, before he was hurled across the alleyway and dashed against the bulkhead.

'Then I condemn you to everlasting life,' the inexorable voice slowly faded. 'You will never leave this ship.'

Tegan was sitting on her bunk looking at the photograph of Aunt Vanessa when she heard the knock. 'Go away,' she said, automatically. But it was not Marriner who spoke. 'It's me,' said the Doctor, rather plaintively. Tegan was on her feet and unbolting the door in a flash, and the distress on her face was plain to see.

'What's the matter?' The Doctor quickly closed the door behind him.

'This!' Tegan held up the photograph. 'And this room!'

'They can reproduce anything they see in the mind,' the Doctor said, gravely. 'That's how this ship was made. Out of the minds of the crew. Just as this room was made out of yours. They use human minds as blueprints. And not only human. Ephemeral minds anywhere – from any system, any galaxy.'

'Are they – are they like Time Lords?' Tegan asked in a small voice.

'No. They exist outside time,' the Doctor answered. 'They are Eternals. They exist in eternity. Exist, not live.'

'But why do they move like automatons sometimes?' Tegan wanted to know. 'Why do they look like zombies? Why that blank stare?'

'Emptiness,' the Doctor answered. 'Their minds are empty, used up. They need ideas. From *us*. They're desperate for them.'

Tegan was beginning to feel desperate, too. 'We've got to get away from here!' she said. 'I can't cope with Marriner for much longer. Let's leave!'

The Doctor shook his head firmly. 'Not before we've found out what is at the end of the race' he said. 'I understand how you feel, but I must ask you to stay. We can't risk them finding out about the TARDIS.' His face was grave and anxious as he finished speaking.

In the wheel-house, Striker and Marriner stood motionless and impassive. Then a faint smile curled Striker's lips. 'TARDIS?' he mumured. Marriner's eyes came to life. He was listening.

'They couldn't *do* anything to the TARDIS, could they?' The Doctor's words had Tegan really worried.

'I wouldn't like to risk it,' he answered. 'They have enormous power.'

He had already reached the door by the time Tegan caught up with him. 'What can we do, then?' she asked desperately.

'Try and distract them,' was the reply. 'Give them something to worry about. Even an Eternal can't put his mind to too many things at once.' He opened the door and hurried into the corridor. 'Come on – we've got to find Turlough.'

In the wheel-house the Captain and Marriner slowly turned to each other. They were alert and concentrating. Suddenly their eyes met. 'Now!' Striker ordered. Marriner jumped to a salute. 'Aye, aye, sir.' Then he left the room.

The Doctor and Tegan hurried along, slightly out of breath from their search. Then as they passed the end of a companionway, the Doctor suddenly stopped dead. He had caught sight of a figure lying motionless in the gloom. It was Turlough. He was recovering consciousness and struggling to sit up by the time they reached him.

'What happened?' the Doctor asked with concern, as he helped him to his feet. But Turlough was evasive. 'Nothing. I fell,' he answered, turning away as he spoke, and straightening his shirt collar.

He was not quick enough to prevent Tegan seeing the livid bruises on his neck. 'What are those marks?' she asked, suspiciously. But the Doctor was hurrying them on their way before she could pursue the point. 'Quickly!' his voice was urgent. 'We must get back to the TARDIS.'

Striker was oblivious of the helmsman at the wheel. He no longer stared out into space; his attention was elsewhere, and he seemed to find something very amusing.

Panting slightly, Tegan reached the bottom of the companion-ladder where the Doctor was waiting. A second later Turlough joined them. Then the blackness of the hold enveloped them once more, as they started to feel their way back to the TARDIS. The Doctor had finally given in to his companions' pleading to be allowed to return. The beams from their pocket torches seemed thinner and fainter, but the Doctor went on ahead with apparent confidence.

'It's round here,' he said firmly, leading them past the pile of crates and boxes. But there was no TARDIS. 'Where is it?' asked Tegan in a frightened voice. 'It *was* here,' the Doctor said slowly. Turlough nearly exploded with quiet irritation. 'The TARDIS can't just have disappeared!' The Doctor was silent for a second, then he swore under his breath. It was himself he was angry with. 'The Eternals have learnt about the TARDIS,' he whispered.

'You are right.' The voice came from behind them. As they swung round, the First Officer was revealed in the light of their torches, standing a few inches away. Turlough turned to make a dash for it, but where there had been empty space a moment earlier, the

Second Officer now stood, close enough to touch them.

'Take the woman to Mr Marriner.'

Tegan's struggles were useless, and she was led away. The Doctor's efforts to help her simply resulted in him being held in a painful and extraordinarily powerful grip by the First Officer.

'Please, Doctor,' the smooth voice was unruffled. 'Resistance is futile. And we mean her no harm.'

'What have you have done with the TARDIS?' was all the Doctor would say. The officer released him. 'Follow me,' he ordered, 'You will soon find out.'

Tegan was escorted, politely but firmly, to the locker where the space equipment was kept. They stopped by the pegs where the pressure suits hung and Marriner emerged from the shadows. 'I'm sorry you wanted to leave,' he said in a reproachful voice, as soon as they were on their own. 'Please put on one of these.'

'A space suit! No!' The last thing Tegan wanted was to go out into that enormous void which surrounded them. But Marriner continued, gently but firmly, 'Please. There is so much I wish to show you.'

Striker's face was expressionless as he looked at the two prisoners in front of him. The Doctor's was equally impassive. 'I underestimated you,' he said in a voice as cold as the Captain's. 'You have a greater ability to read minds than I realised.'

Striker seemed amused. 'You helped me. Such was your concern, I could see into your mind as far away as Miss Tegan's cabin. The picture was as clear as if you were standing here.'

'What picture?' The Doctor's heart sank.

'The picture of your ship,' came the answer. 'I

believe you call her the TARDIS. Adrenalin is a most effective energy boost. It was your own fear that gave her to us.'

The Doctor had never felt so desolate, but anger pulled him together. 'What have you done with the TARDIS?' he asked fiercely. 'And where's Tegan?'

'She's on deck,' Striker replied. 'Perhaps you would care to join her.'

An officer held out two of the space suits, and while the Doctor and Turlough were struggling into them, the Captain continued smoothly, 'On deck you will have an interesting view of our competitors. It might help you decide which one is the saboteur.'

The Doctor went on fastening the suit, keeping his voice casual as he asked, 'What are you all competing for?' There was silence. Pretending to concentrate on a buckle, he persevered, 'The whole point of a race is to win something, after all. So what's the prize?'

'Enlightenment.' Striker's melancholy voice rang as he spoke the word. The Doctor and Turlough exchanged a look. 'Enlightenment?' the Doctor asked.

Striker stared into some secret world of his own. 'The wisdom which knows all things,' he said, 'and which will enable me to achieve what I desire most.' Even as the question framed itself in the Doctor's mind, Striker turned away. 'Do not ask, Doctor, I will not tell you.'

Tegan gripped the ship's rail and gazed about her. How could she have thought that space was empty, when it was so full of stars; there were a hundred thousand million suns in the galaxy they were sailing through, some shining with the brilliant whiteness of Rigel in Orion, some blue, some yellow, some red, some dim as glow-worms; there were open clusters, and close-packed globes of stars; there were nebulae, each a shimmering gauze of light; and in the distance the hazy brightness of another galaxy, the great spiral of Andromeda. There were stars all round, even below the hull of the ship. They were floating in a sea of stars.

'It's beautiful, isn't it?' she heard Marriner saying. 'I can see in your mind you find it so.'

Tegan tried to keep her breathing as calm and even as possible, determined not to give in to the mild claustrophobia that the space helmet induced in her.

'You may remove it if you wish.' Marriner as usual knew exactly how she felt. 'The atmosphere is breathable. It's maintained by an invisible energy barrier.' And then, before she realised what he was about to do, he clicked her helmet open. Every nerve in her body jerked as she waited for annihilation, but nothing happened.

'You like giving people shocks, don't you!' she snapped crossly.

'I wanted to show you I was telling the truth,' Marriner said. 'You can trust me now.' He smiled sweetly at her. 'The helmets are simply an extra precaution.' He removed his own helmet as he spoke, and bent closer to look into her mind.

The two figures leaning against the rail were the first thing the Doctor spotted as he and Turlough emerged, and Tegan turned and saw them almost at the same moment. She waved and started to cross the deck. She was saying something, but Turlough suddenly found that he could not hear her. He could hear nothing but a dull booming in his ears, which made him feel as though his head was going to burst. Then, within the terrible pounding, he began to distinguish a voice.

The Black Guardian was speaking. 'Boy . . . boy . . .' it vibrated inside his skull. 'You are doomed . . . you have failed me . . .'

Turlough saw that the Doctor and Tegan had met now – they were looking at the ships lying astern – they were saying something — but still he could not hear. In agony, trying to shut out the dreadful voice, he clapped his hands to his ears and stumbled away. The others did not even notice, they were engrossed in studying the other contestants. Turlough lurched against the ship's railing in pain. 'You will now see my wrath,' boomed inside his head. 'You will live aboard this ship in perpetual torment for the rest of your natural life.'

Turlough screamed.

The others turned, startled. By then he was already climbing the rail.

'No!' the Doctor shouted, and started to run.

Turlough was over the safety-rail by the time the Doctor reached him. He shook off the restraining hand, and, still screaming, hurled himself into space.

7
Man Overboard!

'Man overboard!' the Doctor's cry was taken up by the look-out on the fo'c's'le-head, and there was shouting as several sailors came scrambling up from below. Jackson was the first through the hatch. 'Who is it?' he yelled. 'Where?' Tegan pointed, mutely. A small figure was floating gently in space behind them, and getting smaller every minute as the ship moved away at speed. 'It's Turlough!' the Doctor was unfastening one of the lifebelts as he spoke. In a few seconds he and Jackson had torn it loose and hurled it over the side. Tegan grabbed Marriner's arm and almost shook him.

'Don't just stand there!' she shouted. 'Do something! Stop the ship! Turn back!'

'It would be ridiculous to risk losing the race for an Ephemeral,' came the calm reasonable reply. Tegan could hardly believe her ears. 'You can't just leave him!' she gasped. 'He'll die out there.' Marriner patted her hand. 'It will be over for him quickly,' he said, soothingly, 'His oxygen supply is very small.'

Tegan flung away from him in disgust and hurried to join the others at the rail. They were all staring after the lifebelt as it floated towards Turlough, the line it was attached to snaking out behind. Turlough stretched his arms towards it, and they held their breaths. Then, as it was almost within his grasp, it reached the extent of its line and stopped. Turlough clutched frantically, but ship, line and lifebelt moved relentlessly on, leaving him behind in their wake. Tegan buried her face in her hands, she could hardly bear to watch. A ragged cheer from some of the sailors made her raise her head.

'Look!' Jackson shouted, triumphantly. 'The *Buccaneer*! She's putting her sails back!'

The Doctor made a dive for the telescope, and swung it frantically towards the ship astern. Marriner simply stared in disbelief. 'She can't be!' he said in a surprised voice.

'She is!' came from the Doctor at the telescope. 'She's heaving to!'

To Turlough, drifting hopelessly, the great hull looming over him seemed like a cliff face. From somewhere above, a net floated down and enveloped him. He was already finding it difficult to breathe, and as he felt himself being swung up and saw the side of the ship flashing past him, he lost consciousness.

'He's safe!' the Doctor said, and turning away from the telescope, he hurried towards the hatch. 'Where are you going?' Tegan demanded. But the Doctor was already out of sight. 'To talk to Striker,' his voice floated back up the ladder. 'We must get to that ship.'

Tegan turned to look at the *Buccaneer*, and caught sight of Marriner's puzzled expression. 'Surprising of Captain Wrack,' he commented mildly.

'Surprising?' Tegan blazed at him. 'To save someone's life?'

'To turn aside from the race,' he answered.

'At least Turlough's safe,' she said triumphantly. But Marriner did not seem to share her relief.

'Is he?' he answered in a detached voice. 'Your friend might be better dead than with the captain of that ship.'

Turlough was only vaguely aware of lying on a deck and of faces peering at him. He heard strange voices, but faint and far away through the roaring in his ears. It was all like a nightmare: and when he surfaced and his senses returned to him, it was to find himself being dragged along a companionway by two seamen. They were a ruffianly-looking pair, one with a long scar up his arm, the other with gold ear-rings and broken teeth, and they did not handle him gently. His knees were scraped and bruised before he managed to find his own feet. It was not until then that he took in the man walking ahead of them. He was obviously an officer of some sort, his brocaded coat flashed with gold thread, but it appeared to have belonged once to someone else, for it fitted him poorly. His broad shoulders were nearly bursting the seams. He walked with the lithe power of a black athlete, and even as Turlough noticed the burnished ebony skin and the panther-like tread, the man flung open a door ahead of them. The room into which he was dragged was very different from Striker's. He caught a glimpse of Persian rugs and a negro statue holding a great candelabra, and then he was thrown to the floor. The officer gave him a shove with his boot. 'Crawl!' he said. 'Lick the Captain's boots.' The booted feet were just ahead of him. He raised his eyes to see velvet breeches, a wide sash with a dagger stuck in it, and then, as he came to the face, he got the surprise of his life. Captain Wrack was a woman. She was also beautiful, with white skin and auburn curls, and a smile. 'Just what I've been waiting for,' she said lazily. From an ivory-inlaid table next to her, she picked up a cutlass, unsheathed, with a jewelled hilt. Still smiling, she tested the blade, and then raised it above her head as though to decapitate him. Turlough closed his eyes. He heard it swishing through the air an inch from his ear, but when he looked again, she was smiling even more charmingly. 'The balance is perfect,' she said. Then, as if losing interest in him, she turned to the officer. 'Mansell –' there was sudden authority in her voice, and the man stepped forward smartly. 'For Captain Davey,' she continued, handing him the cutlass ceremonially. 'With my compliments.' And as he took the weapon, she added, 'A handsome gift, don't you think?'

'A staggering jewel – for a rival,' Mansell answered. He smiled — rather strangely, Turlough thought: and then he saw the man's eyes fixed on one of the gems in the hilt, a huge star sapphire.

'May it have as great an impact as my present to the Greek,' the Captain replied, and again the same strange smile passed between her and her officer. Then she was once more brusque and businesslike, 'Deliver it,' she ordered, 'And these.' She picked up several ornate-looking letters from the table and handed them over. 'The invitation for Captain Striker first.'

Both of them turned and looked at Turlough. 'Striker is bound to accept,' Wrack went on. She nodded briefly and Turlough found his arms seized by the two sailors, while the Captain walked over and stood in front of him. 'He can't refuse,' she went on. 'Not when we have live bait. Wriggling on the hook' and she smiled into Turlough's face.

Tegan was leaning over the ship, looking towards the *Buccaneer*. She had caught sight of a flurry of activity

70

on the deck, and was concentrating hard, trying to make out what was going on there, when she was startled by a voice directly behind her.

'Your friend is safe.' It was Marriner speaking. 'We have received a message. I thought you would like to know.'

'Thank you,' Tegan said, as politely as she could. But there was something about the First Mate that she found unnerving, and she was just about to move away when he stepped in front of her.

'I hope you will forgive me for saying so,' he remarked, 'but I have never experienced a mind such as yours before.'

'Really?' Tegan said vaguely, wondering how she could dodge round him. 'Where's the Doctor? I must go to him.' Marriner went on as though she had not spoken. 'I find your mind a fascinating place to be. So full of riches. Of life.' Tegan closed her eyes firmly.

'What are you doing?' there was dismay in his voice now. 'You've killed your thoughts! You're hiding them from me!' But it was impossible to keep her mind a blank for long, and she opened her eyes despairingly, to see Marriner gazing into her face with even greater interest.

'I'd no idea Ephemerals were so entertaining,' he said. 'Perhaps that's why Wrack stopped to pick up your friend.'

Tegan turned her back on him. As she did, she saw that she had been right about the activity on the deck of the distant galleon. A launch from the *Buccaneer* was heading straight towards them.

The Doctor was having little success. All his efforts to persuade the Captain to collect Turlough had so far failed. Striker was adamant. In fact, he had turned the tables and was asking questions himself, wanting to know why Turlough had jumped. 'I've no idea,' the Doctor answered. 'But we must get him back.' Striker simply turned away. 'It was an impulse , that's all,' the Doctor went on, trying to think up some excuse. 'You know how impulsive the young are. No, I don't suppose you do.' He broke off, a ridiculous thought running through his head. 'Can Eternals have an age?' he was wondering to himself, when Marriner came in, an open letter in his hand and Tegan behind him. 'There is to be a reception aboard the *Buccaneer,*' he announced. 'We have received an invitation from Captain Wrack. Delivered by hand.' Mansell stepped into the room, with a brief bow. 'By hand? I am overwhelmed.' Striker was sardonic. 'You will of course decline,' Marriner said. 'Naturally,' and the Captain dismissed their visitor with a gesture. But before Mansell could withdraw, the Doctor had step-ped forward.

'If you would allow us to go, we could collect Turlough,' he said, reasonably. Tegan was much more impassioned. 'Please let us! Please can't we?' she implored.

Striker seemed bored as he gave his consent, the First Mate impassive. But when Mansell had left and the four of them were alone again, save for the helmsman, Marriner turned to Tegan 'I will escort you,' he said. 'With the Captain's permission.'

'I thought you didn't want to go,' Tegan retorted. For a second there was something almost like concern in the Eternal's eyes.

'I think you might need me,' he replied. 'Captain Wrack has strange ideas of entertainment.'

Turlough was chained to the wall, trying not to give

too much away, as Wrack paced round the wheel-house cross-examining him. She was obviously en-joying herself.

'Have you ever seen a man flogged to death?' She stopped just in front of Turlough to ask the question. 'Or keelhauled? Very painful. Ephemerals have such inventive ways of inflicting pain.' Her voice dwelt lovingly on the last word, and then she became businesslike again. 'Now – tell me what you wanted aboard my ship.'

'Why ask?' Turlough said stubbornly. 'I thought you could read minds.'

'Yours is such a devious one, it's fascinating.' She looked into his eyes. 'I should like to peel it away, layer by layer – until there was nothing left,' she added with relish.

Turlough was extremely frightened. He was not quite the coward that he always claimed to be, but he was terrified of pain, and the creature pacing round him was clearly a sadist. 'Perhaps your intention was sabotage?' she cooed again. He shook his head. 'So why *did* you come to me?' Turlough suddenly had a bright idea. 'Because you're going to win the race,' he gabbled. He had obviously said the right thing. Wrack stopped her pacing and looked at him approvingly. 'Am I?' she sounded pleased. 'What makes you so sure?'

'Oh – what other people have said about you.' Turlough invented desperately.

'That I was ruthless perhaps?' She sounded as though she liked the idea, so Turlough agreed. 'Yes – yes, that's right.' Then he decided to embroider a little. 'I'm the same,' he said bravely. 'And I'm very determined – just the same as you. I like to win.'

'You please me,' Wrack said, slowly and reflective-

73

ly. Turlough pressed his advantage. 'I also want to learn the secret of your power,' he went on glibly. The minute the words were out of his mouth, he realised that he had said the wrong thing. Wrack's eyes were like steel. 'Power?' she asked in a cold voice. 'To win, to control, to read minds –' Turlough babbled frantically. And somehow everything was all right again. Wrack smiled. 'Then don't resist,' she said in a honeyed voice. 'Open your mind. Show faith.' She stroked his chains and they glimmered to nothing under her hand. 'Thank you,' Turlough said, in a small voice. He had pins and needles from the uncomfortable position he had been kept in, and he was trying, unobtrusively, to stretch and flex his cramped muscles, when Mansell spoke from the doorway. 'Captain.' The parchment he handed to Wrack clearly contained good news, for she smiled at Turlough with positive delight.

'Your friends have accepted my invitation. They're concerned about you. Isn't that sweet? I look forward to meeting them,' she said, and there was relish in her voice.

8
The Buccaneer

The Doctor knocked impatiently on Tegan's door.
'Hurry up!' he said, for about the fifth time. 'I'm being
as quick as I can!' a muffled protest came from the
cabin. The Doctor sighed and raised his voice even
louder. 'The launch will be alongside in a moment.'
And then there was a click of the knob, the door
opened, and Tegan came out.

But it was a transformed Tegan who stood there.
The pearly satin of the Edwardian ball gown made her
skin seem more lustrous than ever; the low-cut bodice
revealed elegant sloping shoulders, and a diamond
tiara sparkled in her hair. He nodded approval, but
before he could say anything there was a juddering
under their feet and the whole floor started to vibrate.
A jarring impact made Tegan clutch for the door, and
the ship seemed to shudder convulsively. 'We've been
hit!' the Doctor said. 'You mean – we're under fire?'
Tegan gasped. The next minute Marriner hurried
round the corner. 'Quick! Follow me!' he called out.
Something rocked the ship again, so hard that all
three nearly lost their footing. 'The wheel-house!'
Marriner yelled, disappearing from view. And the
Doctor grabbed Tegan's hand and pulled her along
after him.

'Point-and-a-half to starboard . . .' They could hear
Striker shouting directions to the helmsman even

before they reached the door. 'Topgallant's gone, sir!' came from Marriner. And then Striker's voice again. 'Take in more sail!' As they rushed in, Marriner was bawling down the speaking-tube, 'Take in more sail! Batten down the hatches!' Then they caught sight of the port ahead and stopped dead in their tracks. They were in the middle of an asteroid storm. The view through the screen was terrifying: showers of rocks were hurtling towards them at breath-taking speed. A fusillade of small asteroids could be heard hitting the hull of the ship, and every so often there was a thud and a jar as a larger fragment caught them.

'They must know how to avoid a collision!' said Tegan, appalled at the thought of what would happen if a really massive asteroid hit. 'They *must* – with all their technology!'

'They may choose not to use it,' the Doctor replied. 'It might be against the rules of the race.'

Tegan looked at him in blank horror. 'We could be splintered to matchwood!'

'I don't think that worries them,' the Doctor answered. He was looking at Marriner, and as her eyes followed his, she saw that the First Mate was thoroughly enjoying himself. On Striker's face there was a look of ecstasy as he gazed into the teeth of the storm.

At the wheel of the *Buccaneer*, Wrack was alight with the same excitement and pleasure. Turlough, standing at her side, found her enjoyment of the danger quite incomprehensible.

'Captain –' Mansell's urgent voice sounded from the doorway, 'Davey's ship is gaining on us.'

'Good!' Wrack exclaimed, to Turlough's surprise. 'Take the wheel.' And as the officer jumped to obey she went on, 'We'll wait till she's alongside. Be ready to move away from her fast when I activate.' Then she was striding from the room. 'Come with me,' she shouted over her sholder to Turlough.

'Where are we going?' he asked nervously, trotting at her heels down the corridor.

'You wanted to learn the secret of my power,' she said. 'Now is your chance.' And as they reached a companion-ladder, she swung lightly down, deeper still into the bowels of the ship.

It was distinctly uncomfortable in Striker's wheelhouse, and Tegan clutched the Doctor's arm as the ship was jolted about more and more violently.

'What speed are we doing?' she whispered in his ear.

'I don't know,' the Doctor replied, grimly, 'But it's increasing.'

And then Marriner's excited voice broke in, 'Davey's moving up on the *Buccaneer*.'

All eyes swung to the scanner screen, as a massive nineteenth-century clipper sailed into view, clearly gaining on Wrack's much smaller ship ahead.

Turlough half-scrambled, half-fell down yet another ladder. This must be about as far down they could get, he imagined, and looking round, he saw that Wrack had at last stopped. She was standing in front of a heavy door with a 'Danger' sign over it, operating the opening mechanism. Beside the door was a control panel, marked 'Vacuum Shield', and he just had time to notice that she had set the Force Field gauge to 'full', when the door swung open. She paused for a second on the threshold, and Turlough joined her, panting slightly. 'What is this place?' he asked. She turned to him, her face alive and spiteful. 'Would you like to know?' she asked, and in one swift movement, stepped through and slammed the door in his face. He could hear her laughing on the other side, and then silence.

Everyone in the wheel-house was crowded round the scanner screen, except for Striker himself.

'Davey's taking the wind out of her sails,' Marriner shouted back to him.

The asteroid storm had almost died, and they could see clearly. Out in deep space, the clipper was edging ahead of Wrack's ship.

'What's going to happen?' Tegan said quietly to the Doctor.

His face looked grim. 'I fear – disaster,' he replied.

Turlough's ear was pressed to the 'Danger' door, but he had difficulty making out what was going on beyond. He thought he could hear Wrack's voice, in snatches, and then someone else spoke. It was a man. The deep reverberating tones were unmistakable. For a moment of horror, Turlough thought that he recognised them, and then he was flung back against the wall as a distant explosion rocked the ship. It was still being buffeted about, and Turlough was only just recovering himself, when the door opened and Wrack came out. 'What have you done?' he asked, with sick presentiment. Wrack finished securing the door. 'Improved my chances of winning,' she said coolly, and walked away with barely a glance at him.

Striker and the Doctor were at the wheel together, wrestling to keep the ship on even keel, for the explosion had shaken the yacht too. The others gazed at the scanner screen in fascinated horror. The clipper was burning in front of their eyes. Another massive explosion, and she disintegrated, leaving only flames behind. Marriner was the first to recover.

'Davey's gone,' he called to the Captain, in a matter-of-fact voice. 'An asteroid. Looked like a direct hit.' Then catching sight of Tegan's appalled expression, he added rather lamely, 'Accidents will happen.'

'Especially to anyone who challenges Captain Wrack and the *Buccaneer*!' The Doctor's voice made him swing round. 'What do you mean?' he asked, sharply. The Doctor sauntered over to him. 'Have you forgotten the Greek who challenged Wrack's ship?' he asked the First Mate. 'I wonder if the same thing will happen to us.' Marriner seemed interested, but before he could reply, a whistle from the speaking tube sent him hurrying to answer it. When he looked up a second later, it was to address his Captain.

'The launch is waiting, sir,' he said impassively.

The alleyway which led to Wrack's stateroom was brightly lit, and a guard of honour of buccaneers was stationed along it. It was not their drawn cutlasses that alarmed Tegan, but the doors lying open ahead, and the music and conversation which drifted through to them. Wrack's reception was obviously a large affair.

'I'm scared, Doctor,' she said, hesitating slightly.

But the Doctor surged on eagerly, and it was Marriner who answered her. 'You have no need to be,' he said, and his eyes told her that she looked beautiful.

The Doctor was surveying the stateroom when she caught up with him. A hundred candles twinkled from great silver candelabra, glasses clinked and glittered, and the room seemed to be full of people, all talking and laughing together.

'Fascinating!' the Doctor said, surveying the crowd. 'A complete cross-section.'

'Who are they?' Tegan asked. There were Portuguese, wearing doublet and hose; there were Vikings, with long hair and rough beards; there were Chinese, in the stiff silks of the Manchu dynasty; there were people, it seemed, from every period of earth's history, and from every part of the globe.

'The masters of sail!' the Doctor answered. His voice was admiring, but it suddenly changed. 'Only they're not, are they?' he said sharply. 'They're Eternals, like your friend Marriner. Who knows what their true shape is.'

Tegan's mouth dropped open. It had never occurred to her, until this minute, that the Eternals might not always be as they now appeared. 'They can build ships from what they see in human minds,' the Doctor continued. 'Perhaps their human shape comes from the same source. Whatever they are, to them all this is just a game.'

'To pass the time,' Tegan murmured, her thoughts in a whirl.

'To pass eternity,' the Doctor replied softly. And at that moment, Marriner appeared at their side.

'Champagne?' He proffered the tray he was carrying. Tegan took a glass eagerly, longing for something to steady her nerves. 'Orange juice for me,' the Doctor said, helping himself. He did not drink it, however, but stood, looking round the room.

'Your friend isn't here,' Marriner commented.

'I'd noticed,' was the Doctor's laconic reply. But his eyes still moved methodically from group to group in search of Turlough.

'He isn't far,' Marriner interpolated. 'I can sense

his thought patterns.'

The Doctor continued to look around and so did Tegan, until her gaze was held by an arresting figure. The crowd had parted for a second, and she caught sight of a woman, voluptuous in a tight-laced velvet gown, a mass of auburn curls falling to her shoulders. Even as she stared, mesmerised, the woman's heavy-lidded eyes were turned in her direction.

'Who's that?' she asked, fascinated.

'Your host. Captain Wrack.' Marriner answered.

The woman was already moving towards them, two officers at her heels. 'She's beautiful,' Tegan said, admiringly. 'She is also an Eternal,' came the Doctor's soft voice, and he quickly put a hand over Tegan's glass, just as she was about to raise it to her lips. Then Wrack was with them.

'The wine doesn't please you?' she asked, smiling languidly. Marriner murmured politely that it was excellent.

'But we don't have your remarkable constitutions,' the Doctor smiled back.

Wrack laughed. The sound was throaty and sensuous. 'You're too modest, Doctor.' She stared at him, frankly appraising. 'You are remarkable in other ways. For an Ephemeral.' Then she turned to Tegan and smiled at her. 'And you, my dear, are so intriguing, all my guests have been begging to meet you.' She took the girl's arm. 'You'll excuse us . . .' she murmured, and before either of the two men could answer, Tegan was led away to another group. The Doctor sent her an encouraging smile, as she looked back in dismay, then quickly turned to Marriner. 'What about Turlough?' he asked urgently. 'Can you still sense his mind vibration?'

Marriner concentrated. A puzzled frown appeared

on his face. 'Not clearly,' he said.

Turlough had reached the final rung of the last companion-ladder. He was retracing the way that Wrack and he had taken earlier. A minute later he stood in front of the door marked 'Danger'. If the secret of Wrack's power lay behind that door, Turlough was determined to discover it. The party had provided him with the perfect opportunity. As the stateroom filled with guests he had slipped away, and in the confusion of arrivals and greetings, no one had noticed his departure. Cautiously he had descended ladder after ladder, and now his goal was in front of him. His hands trembled slightly with excitement as he set to work on the opening mechanism. There was a series of clicks and then the operation was complete. But the door did not open. He pushed it, but with no success. Determined not to be thwarted at the last minute, he put his shoulders against it and shoved with all his might. The door gave suddenly, with no warning, and Turlough found himself hurtling through into the room beyond. It was dimly lit and empty, and the door swung back behind him. Just in time he managed to recover his balance on the edge of an iron grille! And teetering there, he nearly lost it again, for he saw suddenly that the whole floor of the room was a grid, open to space – and he was looking down between the bars into infinity.

9
The Grid Room

'I've found him.' Marriner spoke slowly, as if in some sort of trance. 'Where is he?' the Doctor asked anxiously. There was a long pause. 'He's very faint . . .' the First Mate sounded faint himself, as though the effort he was making was draining his strength. 'Concentrate,' the Doctor ordered. Marriner withdrew into himself even more, oblivious of the crowded stateroom, his inward eye searching for Turlough's mind. 'He is afraid,' he said in a low voice. Surprisingly, the news seemed to please the Doctor. 'That should sharpen the image,' he said with satisfaction.

'Yes . . .' Marriner's voice grew stronger as he homed in on his objective. 'The grid room . . . I can see into his mind quite clearly . . . he is in the ion chamber . . .'

'Where's that?' the Doctor asked sharply.

'Down . . . down as far as you can go . . .'

The Doctor threw a frantic glance after Tegan. She was smiling and talking to people, but Wrack was leading her further and further away all the time.

'Danger . . .' Marriner's voice was still withdrawn and concentrated. 'The boy's in danger . . . It's open to space . . . There's a vacuum shield . . .'

Tegan was now nowhere to be seen, but the Doctor could hear her laughter from somewhere in the room. In desperation he seized Marriner's arm, and the firm grip seemed to bring the First Mate to himself again, as if his mind had just returned from a journey.

'Look after Tegan,' the Doctor said urgently. And then he turned and hurried from the room.

Turlough crouched by the grid, staring down into space. He had been frozen in the same position for minutes, as if mesmerised. The immensity of it had obliterated everything else; where he was and what he was doing there were totally forgotten. A sound brought him back to reality. It was the slam of a door. Turlough whirled round, panic-stricken, and flung himself towards it. But he was too late. He could hear the locking devices being clicked into position, but although he banged and shouted, whoever was activating them did not hear. In fact, it was one of the officers, who had spotted that the door was not properly secured and was now firmly fastening it. Turlough would have been even more horrified if he had seen what the officer did next, before continuing his rounds. He turned off the vacuum shield. Had Turlough but known it, all he had left now was four minutes, the run-down time built into the mechanism as a safety precaution. After that, the energy barrier between himself and space would cease to exist.

The Doctor was out of breath, but he dared not stop. Marriner's words still rang in his ears. Turlough was in danger. Down another ladder – a race along a corridor – then a junction. 'Which way? Which way?' he muttered to himself. A glimpse of another ladder to the left and he dashed in that direction. 'How much further?' he thought frantically.

With a last frenzied rattle at the handle, Turlough

turned away from the door, almost in tears. Nobody knew where he was, nobody would come to find him, he was trapped! In despair, he pulled the Cube from his pocket. Frightened as he was of the Black Guardian, he was even more frightened of being left alone here. For ever, perhaps! 'Help me . . . please,' he whimpered. And as though he had been waiting, the Black Guardian's image swam faintly into view. 'I warned you, boy!' The deep voice had a threatening note. 'You failed me. You will die.'

'No . . . No, please . . .' Even as the incoherent syllables tumbled from his lips, Turlough knew that they were useless. Prayers and entreaties would have no effect on the Black Guardian. Indeed, his cloaked image was already fading, leaving Turlough more alone than ever.

Marriner kept Tegan continually in view. As Wrack took her from group to group, he sauntered with them, a little distance away, but always within call. Wrack had been right — her guests did find Tegan intriguing. Admiring glances followed her wherever she went. What Marriner did not realise until too late was that, under Wrack's guidance, her triumphal progress was taking her nearer and nearer to an exit. He saw Wrack put a hand on Tegan's arm as they paused near the door and then, just as he was about to step forward, a servant with a tray of drinks got in his way; a group of guests came between him and the two women; and when he looked again, Tegan had gone.

Turlough's hands were bruised from battering against the door, and he was exhausted. Despairingly, he stepped back – and onto the edge of the grid. For a second his foot wavered over one of the openings. It was almost as though something were sucking it down into space, and the pull threw him momentarily off balance. He clutched at the door and pulled himself back. Almost immediately, a red warning light started flashing on and off on the wall by the door and blinking in and out with it were the words, 'VACUUM SHIELD OFF.' The yelps of an audio-alerting system sounded. Turlough looked at the grid beneath his feet with horror. There was a faint swirling motion between the bars, as the energy field started to close down.

The Doctor reached another crossroads. Then, very faintly from the left, he heard a distant siren, like a danger warning. 'This has to be the way!' he muttered, and plunged down the passage in the direction of the signal.

In the ion chamber the audio-alerting system now sounded one continuous wail, and 'VACUUM SHIELD OFF' glared a fixed red. Turlough was pressed against the wall, staring in horror at the floor. The whirlpool beyond the grid was now much stronger, and he could hear a rushing sound. He pulled the crystal Cube from his pocket and almost sobbed into it, 'Please help me, please help me.' There was nothing except a distant voice saying 'Die . . . die . . . die . . .' and in the rushing noise a sound that could almost have been the Black Guardian chuckling. Turlough made his last effort. It was wrenched from him, without thinking. 'Doctor!' he called at the top of his voice. 'Doctor! Help me!' The audio-alert was now one continuous scream and the chuckling, rushing noise grew louder and louder. Turlough shut his eyes. Then suddenly everything stopped. There was total silence. It was broken by the Doctor's voice. 'So that's where you've got to,' it said mildly.

The candles were guttering in Wrack's wheel–house as she led Tegan in. There were empty wine goblets left here and there, and silver platters of half-eaten food, but otherwise the room was empty.

'I thought you were taking me to meet someone,' Tegan said, suddenly wary.

'They seem to have gone.' Wrack answered with plausible charm, but Tegan felt her suspicions growing. 'Shall we return to the party, then?' she said firmly, and turned towards the door. Wrack raised no objection. 'Whatever you wish.' She sounded perfectly agreeable, but she paused, as though on an afterthought. 'First –' she said, and then broke off. 'What?' Tegan wanted to know. Wrack smiled at her.

'Have you heard of time standing still?'

Tegan was puzzled and thrown off her guard. 'Well . . . yes . . .' she said. 'It's an expression . . . it means . . .' But she never got any further.

'. . . exactly what it says,' Wrack went on, and moved her hand in front of Tegan's face in a soft gesture. The girl stood like a statue, her lips slightly parted on the next word, as though turned to stone in the middle of speaking. Wrack looked into her eyes, and then stepped back and surveyed the motionless figure with satisfaction. 'You will remain frozen in time until I have finished with you,' she said. 'Foolish Ephemeral!'

Turlough opened his eyes at the sound of the Doctor's voice. He could have collapsed with relief as he saw the Time Lord standing in the doorway. 'Vacuum shield!' was all he managed to get out, in a sort of croak. 'I re-set it,' the Doctor answered calmly, and stepping into the room, he closed the door firmly behind him. Why the knowledge that he was safe should make him feel like passing out, Turlough could not understand. Reaction, he imagined. 'I thought I was going to die,' he heard himself saying feebly. 'Not yet.' The Doctor's voice was kindly, but he seemed more interested in the grid room than in Turlough. 'What are you doing in here?' he asked rather absently, as he prowled around looking at everything. 'Something Wrack told me,' Turlough managed to get out. 'She said this place contained the secret of her power.'

'Did she?' The Doctor sounded interested, but he still went on with his examination. 'It is part of the ion drive system, of course.'

'Why is it open to space?' Turlough asked. He thought with horror of that gigantic vacuum in which he had so nearly disintegrated. The Doctor's reply was brief and to the point. 'Better reception' was all he said. And then suddenly he stopped dead, looking at something on the grid at his feet. He looked next at the ceiling overhead, and gave a low whistle. 'What is it?' Turlough asked. There was an urgent note in the Doctor's voice as he answered. 'Wrack uses this place as a receiver for something else as well. Something quite different.' 'What?' Turlough's curiosity was so strong that he crossed over to the dreaded grid again without even hesitating. 'Look at that.' The Doctor pointed to the floor where they were standing. Unlike the squared pattern of the rest, the girders at that point formed the shape of an eye. The Doctor pointed directly overhead. In the ceiling above them was a small eye-shaped aperture, a crystal at the centre of it – like a pupil – from which a dim light filtered. 'Know what it is?' he asked.

Turlough was nonplussed. 'It looks like an eye,' he said, hesitantly. The Doctor's voice sounded grim. 'Only in appearance' he replied. 'It functions as a massive amplifier.' Turlough had a moment's sudden clarity. 'That's what Wrack uses to destroy the ships!' he exclaimed. The Doctor nodded. It was almost with a feeling of disappointment that Turlough went on, 'So that's the secret of her power!'

'Not quite,' the Doctor's voice sounded grave. 'This is only part of it. We still have to locate the focus.'

'What d'you mean?' Turlough asked.

The Doctor spoke slowly, as though thinking aloud. 'Wrack is only a channel for the power. And she must have something to focus it on. A focus aboard every ship she plans to destroy. Otherwise it wouldn't work. Now how do you think she manages it?' And he looked at Turlough as though expecting some sort of answer.

Wrack unlocked a small heavy coffer on one of the tables. She lifted the lid and looked inside, then looked at Tegan, standing immobile at the other side of the room, the light shining on her tiara. From the coffer she lifted a large jewel, a cabuchon crystal. She looked again towards the girl, and her amusement was not a pleasant thing to see.

The Doctor was still staring at the eye of the amplifier. It reminded him of something, but he could not think what. Then Turlough interrupted his train of thought. 'How big would this point of focus have to be?' he asked. The Doctor indicated a size between his thumb and index finger. 'No bigger that that,' he said, and immediately it came to him. 'Of course!' He could see it in his mind's eye. 'The clasp! That's why it was out of period!' And he made for the door. Turlough followed him. 'What are you talking about?' he demanded. The Doctor did not even pause. 'Critas the Greek,' he said, his hand on the opening lever. Turlough still did not understand. 'You mean the first ship that blew up?' he asked. 'Yes!' The Doctor finally did stop, in exasperation. 'Wrack gave him a jewelled clasp. As a present. It must have been from her. And somehow she worked the same sort of trick with Davey.'

'She did!' Turlough exclaimed. He had a sudden vision of the cutlass blade swishing past his ear, and the hilt with the star sapphire. 'She gave him a sword! There was a jewel like a crystal – in the handle!'

'That was it!' the Doctor said, triumphantly.

Turlough had a sudden sick feeling. 'Will she try the same thing with Striker?' he asked.

'I shouldn't think so!' The Doctor still sounded pleased. 'I can't see Striker or Marriner accepting anything from Wrack. They don't trust her.'

Turlough felt quite euphoric. 'Luckily for us!' he enthused. But the Doctor's face had clouded again. 'That won't stop her,' he said. 'She'll find a way.'

Carrying the crystal carefully, Wrack crossed the room and held it up to the tiara in Tegan's hair. Matter was malleable in the hands of an Eternal, and when she lowered them again they were empty. The crystal remained, set perfectly in the centre of the tiara. Its shape and size were exactly that of the ruby in Critas's clasp, the sapphire in the hilt of Davey's sword, the pupil in the eye of the amplifier. Wrack stepped back and surveyed her creation. 'Perfect!' she said, with a little laugh.

10
Spy!

To Turlough's surprise, the Doctor stopped suddenly at the door of the ion chamber.

'Before we leave,' he said, 'we must work out some sort of plan.'

Turlough could hardly believe his ears. 'Here!' he complained, looking apprehensively at the grid and at the panel of warning signals, now blessedly quiet. 'Let's get out of this place! We don't want to hang about making plans in *here!*' The Doctor stayed put. 'We do' he said. 'This is the best place. They're far less likely to pick up our mind vibration at this level.' Turlough sighed in exasperation. 'All right, what d'you think we ought to do, then?' he asked, grumpily. The Doctor gave him a searching look. 'I've got to think of some way of staying on this ship . . .'

'You want to stay!' Turlough exclaimed in amazement. 'Why?'

'Because I've got to stop Wrack winning this race somehow. Any ideas?' Again the Doctor gave him the same long questioning look. An idea *was* beginning to form in Turlough's mind, though it may not have been quite the sort that the Doctor envisaged. Turlough was thinking of a way to have his cake and eat it.

'Let *me* stay,' he said. And then, as the Doctor did not respond, he added in an aggrieved voice, 'Or don't you trust me yet?'

'You couldn't cope.' The Doctor was kind but firm. 'These creatures have vast powers. That's why none of them must win. To achieve further power would be disaster.' And as though that was his final word, the Doctor started opening the door.

'But what about the other ships?' Turlough could not help exclaiming. 'We can't stop *all* of them winning.'

The Doctor smiled at him. 'We can try,' he said.

And then the door was at last open, and they walked out into the safety of the corridor – and straight into the arms of Mansell and two officers. There was no time to think of excuses. Without a word, the two officers grabbed the Doctor. He struggled, briefly, while Turlough watched, paralysed with fright. But he was no match for the power of the Eternals, and very soon they had him pinned to the floor. Mansell's cutlass was an inch from his throat. 'Resist further and you will regret it,' the buccaneer said. His expression seemed to indicate that he personally would positively enjoy the bloodshed to follow.

Tegan stood silent and still. There was not the slightest movement from a ribbon on her gown, or a stray wisp of hair. She did not even seem to breathe. Wrack sauntered over and surveyed her. She looked at the crystal gleaming in the centre of the tiara, and then she said pleasantly, 'Where were we? Oh yes – Have you heard of time standing still?' and she snapped her fingers. Immediately Tegan clicked out of her frozen state and went on talking as though nothing had happened.

'. . . Yes . . . It's just an expression. It means – '

She suddenly broke off and looked around her. 'Why have you brought me here' she asked. Everything seemed strangely disconnected, as though she had just woken from a dream.

'I wanted you to meet someone, but they seem to have gone,' Wrack smiled at her. There was something gloating in those heavy lidded eyes that Tegan did not care for. 'I'd like to rejoin the party please,' she said, rather haughtily. Wrack's smile grew blander. 'Of course,' she purred. And then, with a sly sideways look, she added, 'And *I* would like to speak to the Doctor. The image of him in your mind is quite intriguing.'

There was no sign of the Time Lord in the state-room. Tegan stood in the entrance, surveying the scene, Wrack at her side.

'I can't see him anywhere,' she said anxiously.

'But there is Marriner,' the other woman murmured in her ear. 'Longing for your company.'

Tegan was not interested. All she wanted to do was find the Doctor. But Wrack watched the young man pushing his way eagerly towards them through the crowd, and she seemed amused. 'Don't let me detain you,' she whispered, and moved away, a second before the First Mate arrived at Tegan's side.

'I've been looking for you everywhere,' he said urgently. 'I was worried. Where did Wrack take you?'

Tegan found his concern slightly irritating. 'To the wheel-house.' She tried to sound as noncommittal as possible, but Marriner was not diverted. 'You're unharmed?' he asked, even more fiercely. Tegan gave him a bored look. 'Of course.' Marriner made the mistake of inexperience – he tried to explain himself. 'I – I was concerned for you,' he muttered. For the first time, Tegan felt that she could cope. There had been other young men boringly concerned about her in the past. She was on home ground.

'Thank you. You needn't have been' she said, dismissively.

The squelch did not work on Marriner. He ignored it, and simply continued to state his own feelings, which appeared to be quite impassioned.

'I missed you' he said, hotly. 'I was concerned.' He looked into her eyes. 'I am empty without you.'

That was enough for Tegan. 'Please go away,' she said firmly.

But none of her usual ploys seemed to work. Marriner still went on. 'You are life itself. Without you, I am nothing. Don't you understand?' Tegan stirred uneasily. She did hate emotional scenes, particularly when she could not return the emotion. 'What?' she murmured vaguely. Marriner held her arm. 'I'm empty. You give me being.' His voice shook with passion. 'I look into your mind and I see life, I see energy, excitement. I want them. I want you. Your thoughts shall be my thoughts, and your feelings my feelings.' Tegan decided that this time she really had got out of her depth. She tried to sound as blasé as possible as she said, dampingly, 'Wait a minute, hang on – are you trying to tell me you're in love with me?' Marriner's face went blank. 'Love?' he said, as though he had never heard the word before. 'What is love?' And then his urgency returned and he looked into her eyes and said, longingly, 'I want existence.'

The Doctor and Turlough were being marched along under guard, when round a corner they came face to face with Wrack. Mansell saluted. 'I found them coming out of the grid room,' he reported. Then, before anyone could stop him, Turlough suddenly shook off the hands holding him, stepped forward, and pointed at the Doctor. 'He's a spy!' he said, accusingly. The Time Lord looked at him with surprise, and for a second they stared at each other in silence. Then Turlough turned to Wrack.

'I saw him wandering around and followed him,' he said plausibly.

Mansell, at least, was not easily taken in. 'What were you doing in the grid room?' he rapped.

'I followed him in,' came the innocent reply.

'Why didn't you summon help?'

'From where?' Turlough was a good liar. 'I was trying to apprehend him myself, when you found me.'

Wrack had been listening to this exchange with interest. Now ignoring both of them, she stepped up to the Doctor and looked, long and hard, into his face.

'Spying, Doctor?' she asked sweetly.

'I'd hardly call it spying.' The Doctor kept his tone as mild as possible in an attempt to play down the situation. 'We were welcomed as guests – given the freedom of the ship.'

'You think freedom extends to a door marked "Danger"?' Wrack was equally conversational, but there was a hidden menace in her words. She smiled at Turlough. 'What should I do with your friend the spy?' she asked, companionably. They both looked at the Time Lord. Turlough did not even hesitate. 'Get rid of him,' he said in an expressionless voice. Wrack seemed intrigued.

'How?' she asked, as though torn between several delicious choices. Turlough's composure faltered, and he almost stammered as he hurried to explain, 'I meant – send him back. Send them all back. To Striker.'

Wrack gave him a melting look. 'And what about you?' she asked softly.

The guard of honour was still presenting cutlasses, still standing at attention, as Tegan and Marriner emerged from the stateroom and looked down between the long lines of buccaneers. Two officers had interrupted Marriner's conversation with her, somewhat to Tegan's relief, and asked them both to leave. There had been no explanation, but even Marriner did not attempt to argue. Had the men been mere Ephemerals, he would have dealt with them, but they were creatures of his own kind, with equal powers. There was obviously some urgency about their departure, for Tegan was almost hustled into the passage. 'All right, all right – don't push!' she protested, shaking off the hand of the officer who was trying to hurry her along. At almost the same moment, she caught sight of the Doctor, waiting in Mansell's custody. 'Where's Turlough?' she asked, running over to him. The Doctor did not reply, simply gave a warning glance in the direction of his captor.

'You will board the launch now,' the tall buccaneer said, impassively.

'What about Turlough?' Tegan whispered into the Doctor's ear.

'He's staying,' came the whisper back.

And Mansell spoke again. 'The launch. Now.'

It was clearly a final order, and the two officers drew their swords.

'Come on,' the Doctor said breezily, and started off down the passage. The rest of the cortège fell in behind. By walking slightly more quickly than the others, Tegan managed, apparently casually, to catch up.

'You can't let them keep him!' she hissed.

'He wants to stay,' the Doctor was as emphatic as he could be out of the corner of his mouth.

Tegan was nothing if not persistent. 'Why?' she asked through closed lips, like a ventriloquist. The Doctor halted, pretending that he had dropped something. And as they both searched for the imaginary object on the floor, he muttered, 'Wrack mustn't win the race. He's stayed to prevent her.'

Tegan forgot to keep her voice down. 'What!' she exclaimed, 'You can't believe *that!*'

'Sh!' came from the Doctor.

But it was too late. Mansell towered over them. 'Move!' he said, stonily.

Wrack was pouring a pale golden wine into the silver goblets. She poured carfully, ignoring Turlough. She sipped, just as carefully, and a look of pleasure crossed her face. 'Muscatel,' she murmured, and turned sleepy eyes to the boy, as he stood watching her dejectedly from the doorway. 'The grapes are grown in an island in the ocean – the Atlantic, I believe they call it on that planet. Its taste was buried deep in the mind I took it from. He was a Captain too – of a ship like this. A buccaneer. I had to dig deep to get it' – she smiled, cruelly – 'Very deep. I'm afraid I hurt him.'

'Wh-where is he now?' Turlough asked.

'I had no more use for him,' Wrack answered, and held out a goblet. 'Drink.'

It sounded more like a command than an invitation, and Turlough took the proffered wine and drank, trying hard not to think of the wretched buccaneer whose mind had unwittingly provided it.

Wrack wandered over to a divan in the corner of the room. 'Your friends have gone,' she commented idly, sinking down amongst the cushions.

'Good riddance.' Turlough mustered as much bravado as he could.

97

Wrack beckoned him over. 'My thanks for detecting the spy,' she said, smiling up into his face. 'And for choosing to stay with me.' She patted the divan next to her, and Turlough sat down, beginning to feel pleased with himself. Her next remark caught him off guard. 'Why did you?' she asked.

'I told you,' Turlough thought quickly. 'I like to be on the winning side.'

Wrack seemed amused. 'And you want a share of the winnings?' Turlough nodded. 'Even if you're not sure what they are?'

Turlough's mouth set in a stubborn line. 'I know what the prize is,' he said. 'Enlightenment.'

'And you know what that means of course.'

He had a sneaking feeling that Wrack was laughing at him, but as she got up and started to pace the room, still talking, he realised that she was completely carried away by her plans, and hardly conscious of his presence.

'When Enlightenment is mine,' she said, 'I will no longer depend on Ephemeral minds. Everything conceived, from the beginning of time to the end, will be clear to me.' Her eyes glowed. 'I shall create and destroy as I wish. I shall never be bored again.'

'So Enlightenment brings knowledge, is that it? Or is it power?' Turlough felt completely fuddled.

'Enlightenment brings whatever one desires,' Wrack said. 'I desire to be amused.' She crossed to one of the portholes. 'And I have a new toy to show you.' She beckoned to him. 'Come and see how I entertain my guests.'

Standing at her side, he looked down onto the deck below. Several of the crew were rigging something up over the side of the ship, under the direction of two officers. 'What are they doing?' he asked curiously.

And then as they stepped back to survey their work, he knew. A long flat board was lashed there, sticking out into space, a pathway to nothing.

'The plank,' Wrack said. 'An ingenious Ephemeral idea for disposing of those who stand in one's way.'

There was a certain amount of jostling and ribald laughter from the buccaneers below. More of them appeared, and then the crowd parted, to form a rough lane leading back to the companion-ladder. With a sick feeling, Turlough saw that several of the guests had been dragged up and were cowering in a frightened group by the hatch. As he watched, one of them, a Spanish officer, was pushed forward between the two lines of buccaneers. There were jeers and guffaws as he was dragged to the edge of the plank and forced to climb onto it. He took a few trembling steps and tried to turn back, but a cutlass point prodded him on. Another guest was dragged into view to take his turn. And at that moment the Spaniard's weight tilted the plank downwards and he started slipping. Screaming and slithering frantically, he fell. But as he went into space, the scream was cut short and the man seemed to vanish. The buccaneers lining the deck cheered and clapped, and so did Wrack in the wheel-house. Turlough, alone, was silent.

'Does it distress you?' asked Wrack, with a mocking glance.

Turlough was shocked, but it was amazement rather than distress that filled him. 'What happened to him?' he gasped.

'He is out of the race,' Wrack smiled.

'But – but the pressure –' Turlough stuttered. 'It's a vacuum – he should have disintegrated – exploded – he just – disappeared –'

'He is an Eternal,' Wrack answered. 'Like me. We

do not exist in Time, so there is no moment of time that can see us cease to be. We are beyond sequence.'

Turlough shook his head in bewilderment.

'They will all survive,' she went on in a bored voice. 'Merely transfer. You Ephemerals are different. You die so easily.'

She turned to him with a smile. 'Shall we see? One of the crew, perhaps?' Turlough shook his head, unable to speak. 'No?' There was mocking disappointment in Wrack's voice. And then a burst of shouting from the buccaneers below made him look down again. They were all staring up at the wheel-house, a sea of grinning faces.

'Shall we join them on deck?' Wrack asked, some secret amusement in her voice.

'Why?' Turlough stared at her blankly.

'They're waiting for you.'

The smile on her face was so evil that Turlough knew at once what she meant.

'No! No – you don't understand!' he gasped. And before he knew where he was, Mansell and a second officer had grabbed him. He struggled violently, but they held him firm, and Wrack walked over and looked at him.

'I understand very well,' she said. 'The Doctor was not the only spy.'

'I wasn't spying!' The cry was wrenched from Turlough.

'You forget – I can see into an Ephemeral mind. Even a murky one such as yours.'

'But I'm on your side,' he protested desperately. 'I just wanted a share – just some of the prize.'

'You wanted it all!' There was contempt in Wrack's voice. 'Your mind is divided – confused – hard to read sometimes. But there is one thing clear in it always.

Greed.' She turned her back. 'Take him away. He bores me.'

Turlough started struggling again, but he was dragged inexorably towards the door. 'No – no, listen –' he gasped, straining frantically to gain her attention – to convince her – to make her change her mind. 'I heard – When I was outside the ion chamber – I heard it – the Power that speaks to you. I heard – and I know the voice!'

Wrack turned and looked at him. And Turlough tried a last desperate throw.

'He speaks to me as well,' he gasped. 'I serve him. As I will serve you.'

The men released him, and crumpling to his knees, he grovelled on the floor at Wrack's feet.

11
Focus Point

'I'm going to change' Tegan said, crossly. 'I've had about enough of this outfit.' She glared at Marriner, swept into her cabin and banged the door behind her. She also bolted it, and then leant back against it with a sigh of exhaustion. She wanted no more of Marriner prying into her mind and into her feelings. 'He's like a leech!' she shuddered to herself. She thought about the Doctor and felt even crosser. How *could* he imagine that Turlough was staying on that ship to *stop* the buccaneers winning? Turlough was simply out for his own advantage, and if the Doctor could not see that . . . Her thoughts broke off in a jangle, and she yanked fiercely at the fastenings of her dress.

In the passageway outside, the two men exchanged a look. 'Women!' was what the Doctor's seemed to say, with puzzled affection. Marriner cleared his throat:

'I must report to the Captain. We're nearly into the final leg.'

The Doctor watched him hurry away, and then knocked on the door. 'I'm going to the wheel-house,' he called in a mollifying voice.

There was silence for a second. But Tegan sounded her usual self when she spoke again. 'I'll join you in a moment.' Her silk stockings and the high-heeled silken slippers were scattered about the floor. The

103

flurried heap of lace on the bed was her petticoat. A second later it was joined by her dress. Then her tiara. The band of diamonds lay where she had thrown it, glittering against the satin of her ball gown. At the centre of its filigree work, the cabuchon glowed brightest of all.

The Doctor caught up with Marriner just as they reached the wheel-house. The distant shouts from the rigging had been growing more and more excited. And, as they burst through the door together, the Doctor could see why. Far ahead of them, through the port, shone a ring of lights, like a harbour floating in space. Striker turned to greet them, his face triumphant.

'The Enlighteners!' he said. 'We are nearly there, gentlemen.'

The whole ship seemed to be full of bustle and excitement to Tegan. She could hear a shanty from the men hauling on the ropes, she could hear the bosun's pipe, and could hear shouting from the look-out. As she burst into the wheel-house, the loudest voice of all was the Captain's.

'More sail, Mr Mate!' Striker was yelling. 'Cram on everything she's got!'

'What's happening?' Tegan wanted to know.

'The race is nearly over,' the Doctor whispered back to her.

Marriner looked up from shouting instructions down the speaker-tube. 'We're pulling away!' he crowed. A wintry smile appeared on Striker's face. 'We'll show her a clean pair of heels,' he said with satisfaction. But as the First Mate turned back to relay the orders, he suddenly stopped dead. 'Captain!' he grated. 'Look!' All eyes followed his, as he stared at the scanner screen and Wrack's ship pictured there.

'They've hoisted their moonrakers,' the Doctor said softly. Every mast of the *Buccaneer* seemed to have blossomed. She had mounted sail even above her topgallants, and she scudded now under full canvas.

There was laughter in Wrack's voice. 'A surprise for Captain Striker,' she gloated. Mansell grinned back at her from the wheel. 'We're gaining on them!' But his captain was suddenly serious and her eyes burnt with strange intensity, as she rapped out, 'I want us lying level!' Mansell nodded. Obviously the order was important in some way, for his hands tightened on the wheel and he went back to his task with renewed concentration. Wrack turned to Turlough. He had not been hustled to the plank with the other victims, his passionate plea had succeeded. Wrack had kept him at her side ever since, but she had not spoken to him again until this moment.

'You wish to serve me. Come. We will go to the great Power who aids us, and together we will listen to his voice.'

And with these words she hurried from the room.

'Wrack's still moving up on us!' Striker's voice sounded grim. There was the same note in Marriner's as he shouted 'break out that skysail!' into the speaking-tube.

Tegan was puzzled. 'What *are* moonrakers?' she whispered to the Doctor. He seemed as worried as the officers as he muttered back, 'Pirate sails. For speed. With those, they're faster than we are.'

Tegan could hardly believe her ears. 'You mean — they'll be able to overtake us?' she gasped.

The Doctor nodded sternly, but Marriner's next

words sent her spirits flying up again. 'Wrack's level – but we're holding her!' he shouted.

The news did not seem to cheer the Doctor. 'They can pass us any time they want to,' he said fatalistically.

'Then why don't they?' Tegan snapped. It wasn't like the Doctor to be so pessimistic. But his gloom lifted suddenly and he looked at her as though she had said something very interesting. 'Why don't they indeed!' he said slowly.

'We're still holding level with her,' came Marriner's voice.

And then the Doctor went into action. 'No!' he shouted, loudly and urgently, and rushed up to the Captain and Marriner. 'No – you've got it the wrong way round! It's Wrack who's holding level with *us*! She's positioned! She's moved in for the kill!'

Outside the 'Danger' door, Wrack was setting the force field control, Turlough at her elbow. She stepped back. 'Now. Open it,' she ordered. Turlough's palms were sweating and his hands shook as he moved the lever and pushed the heavy door open. Wrack went on into the empty grid room, and after a second's hesitation, he followed her.

The Doctor was talking fast and frantically. He was not sure how much Striker and the First Mate believed him, but he had to convince them.

'I tell you that's how Wrack was positioned when the Greek ship exploded,' he said desperately. 'She was lying level! And when Davey's was destroyed! She was practically alongside him! Don't you remember?'

Neither seemed to be paying any attention. Striker

went on shouting for more sail. But Marriner suddenly turned away from the speaking-tube. 'That's everything we've got,' he said in quiet desperation, and looked to the Doctor, as though asking him for something.

'We can't pull away from her,' the Time Lord responded grimly. 'She's got us where she wants us!' But a second later he lifted his head, and the old fighting light was back in his eyes. 'The Focus!' he said, with sudden inspiration. 'We must find the Focus.'

Tegan and Marriner looked at him in bewilderment.

'She must have managed it!' he said to them irritably, as though they were half-wits. 'She must have got it aboard somehow!' And then as Tegan looked at him blankly, he almost shook her. 'Did she give you anything?' he asked frantically. 'When we were aboard her ship? Anything at all? *Think*!'

'No!' the girl exclaimed defensively, tears pricking behind her eyelids. But it was not anger that was making the Doctor shout, it was sheer frustration. 'It's here somewhere! It has to be!' he said, letting her go and looking wildly round the room. Tegan began to think he was having some sort of brainstorm. '*What* has to be here?' she asked.

'The point of Focus!' the Doctor's voice was long-suffering. 'Without it, the power she channels is useless!'

Marriner decided to take a hand. 'What power?' he asked, only half-believing.

But there was something in the Time Lord's voice that convinced him, as he answered softly, 'The power of darkness'.

Wrack picked her way, sure-footed, to the centre of the

grid. Turlough watched her from the doorway with a thumping heart. Wrack stood motionless for a second, and then slowly raised her arms and looked upwards. As she stared into the eye-shaped opening above her, the crystal that was its pupil slowly seemed to darken. From where Turlough stood, it was as if a beam, not of light, but of blackness, enveloped her. All that he could see was her pale face, floating as though disembodied. And the whole room grew dimmer.

'What would this Focus *look* like?' Tegan felt desperate. 'It could be anything!' the Doctor said irritably. But he stopped flinging himself around the wheelhouse and peering into corners and examining nautical instruments, and he looked at her again as though she had a reasonable degree of intelligence.

'Probably a crystal of some sort,' he went on. 'So big, perhaps,' he held up his fingers in measurement. 'Could be part of a jewel. A clasp – the hilt of a sword –' The expression on Tegan's face stopped him. 'Part of a jewel?' she said, in an odd voice.

The grid room was darker still. Wrack called to some strange invisible power, and as she intoned, her voice became more distant and echoing, until finally it died away. In the silence that followed, her face seemed to change. It contorted until it was almost unrecognisable. Then the lips moved again, mouthing silently at first, until a voice filled the room. 'I am here.' It was not Wrack's voice, but a man's, speaking through her mouth. With a gulp of terror, Turlough knew that he had been right. It was the voice of the Black Guardian.

The Doctor hurried ahead, Tegan and Marriner in his wake. Tegan was still talking, although rather breathlessly.

'I thought it seemed different when I took it off,' she panted. 'That was what had changed! It was there – like a diamond – right in the centre of the tiara!'

'What happened when you were in the wheel-house with Wrack?' the First Mate asked, keeping pace easily at her side.

'Nothing – I can't think–' Tegan felt her head beginning to whirl.

'Come on!' the Doctor shouted, and disappeared round a corner ahead.

Turlough watched in horror, mesmerised by that pallid face floating in the gloom. The beam of darkness grew more Stygian still, and still the deep voice, reverberated.

'Focus . . . focus . . . Your mind is a channel . . . through which power will flow . . . focus your mind . . .'

In Tegan's cabin, the tiara was lying on the bed where she had thrown it. But the crystal which shone at its centre was changing. It was darkening. And it was beginning to throb.

Tegan's lungs felt as though they were bursting. When she saw the Doctor stop, she thought at first that he must need a breather too. But he simply opened the glass door of a fire-prevention cabinet on the wall, grabbed an axe from inside, and ran on. Tegan moaned with exhaustion. Then, ignoring Marriner's sympathetic glance, she pulled herself together, and with a colossal effort, flung herself forward again.

On the bed, the crystal in the tiara was darker still. It

was pulsing faster... and faster...

Wrack's lips moved, but the voice had sunk to a whisper, hissing in the darkness. 'Focus . . . focus . . . focus . . .'

The crystal was now coal-black, with a life of its own. Its pulse filled the room like a drumming noise, and in the beats sounded the Black Guardian's sibilant voice, 'Focus . . . focus . . . focus . . .'

There was a crash as the door was flung open, and the Doctor dashed in. Without even pausing, he grabbed the tiara from the bed and hurled it on the floor. When Tegan and Marriner arrived, he was slashing at it with the axe. They gaped at him, appalled, as the throbbing in the room grew louder and more insistent. And then the Doctor was on target. A blow from the axe caught the crystal and smashed it into fragments. For one moment of blinding relief, he thought he had succeeded. But, to his horror, each of the fragments seemed to take up the beat, each pulsed darkly, each one became a Focus. The voice became several voices, overlapping, whispering. 'Focus . . . focus . . .'

In the darkness of the grid room, Turlough stared in terror as Wrack's face, pale in the gloom, multiplied into many faces, like the heads of a Hydra, all whispering . . .

'What is it? What's happening to it?' Tegan gasped appalled.

'I can't destroy it!' The Doctor was furious with himself. 'I'm a fool! Its power has multiplied!' He glanced frantically around the room, and grabbed the first thing he saw. It was a flimsy scarf of Tegan's, lying over the back of a chair. Frantically, he started shovelling the pieces of crystal into it.

'Help me!' he panted 'I've got to get rid of it!'

Tegan and Marriner dropped to their knees, scrabbling urgently for the black fragments pulsing on the floor. The minute they were all collected, the Doctor was on his feet and twisting the scarf into a bundle, he dashed from the room with it clutched in his hand. The other two hurried after him. Along passages they ran, up ladders, along more passages – Tegan thought she was going to collapse.

'Where's he going?' she gasped, with a stitch in her side.

'The deck!' Marriner answered, grabbing her hand and pulling her along. 'All the portholes are sealed –'

The top companion-hatch was flung open and the Doctor almost fell through on his last legs. He tried to stagger to the rail, but collapsed, the bundle in his hand buzzing like a swarm of bees. Driven on by desperation, he crawled across the deck. Still holding the bundle, beating now to a crescendo, he dragged himself to his feet, and with one last effort, hurled it over the rail. Out into space it went, in a great arc. And as Marriner reached the top of the ladder, there was a blinding flash of white light, and it exploded.

12
The Prize

The Doctor, Tegan and Marriner lay on the deck, completely winded. Even Marriner's body had responded to the sprint as though it were human.

'Just in time,' the Doctor murmured. The wood of the deck felt warm under his hands and he relaxed. He could even have gone to sleep, if Marriner had not started talking. He was the first of the three to recover, and as he got up, his eyes sparkled with interest.

'Fascinating!' he said. 'For an Ephemeral to outwit an Eternal!' He was almost speechless with admiration for a moment. 'I would have thought it an impossiblity!'

Rage restored the Doctor, more than any amount of resting would have done. 'An impossibility?' he exclaimed, leaping to his feet. 'Not at all!'

Marriner looked at him as though he were a clever pet of some sort. 'We have complete control over matter,' he said, in a voice that practically patted the Doctor on the head. 'Had you merely *imagined* the Focus as being jettisoned out there in space, I could have converted the image into reality. We would not have needed to expend so much physical effort.'

'Why *didn't* you do it, then!' Tegan snapped.

'Because he didn't think of it.' The Doctor dismissed Marriner with a look, and turned back to Tegan. 'They're far more dependent on us than we are on them,' he said. 'Without us, they're empty nothings!'

His eyes had their old look of self-reliance again. He had found the Eternals' measure. But suddenly he lifted his head, almost like a horse sniffing the air. Marriner seemed to sense something too. They stood motionless for a second, neither of them speaking.

'What is it?' Tegan whispered. She knew there was something different, but she could not quite place what it was. Then she realised. Everything was still. The pennant at the masthead had stopped flapping. The sails hung limp.

'The wind,' the Doctor said softly. 'It's dying.'

In the ion chamber the beam of darkness had disappeared and the whole room had grown lighter. Wrack still stood at the centre of the grid, but seething with anger. When she spoke again, the voice that came from her lips was her own, but it was venomous.

'Striker's ship is still whole,' she spat.

It was not until that moment that Turlough realised which ship she had been about to destroy. He should have known, he told himself. Watching her, almost sick with relief, he felt that she could actually sense the other ship's existence. Just as a moth can detect the presence of a female of its kind up to thirty miles away, from a molecule of its scent in the air, so Wrack was aware of the other minds aboard that ship. If her plan had succeeded, they would have flashed the images of their own destruction to her, and then their messages would have ceased completely. But the living picture-show was still going on, and she knew that she had failed.

The door burst open and Mansell hurried in. 'Captain –' was the only word he managed to get out, before she rounded on him.

'I know!' her eyes blazed. 'Striker's ship still exists.'

'But becalmed! The wind has dropped.' His voice was ingratiating, and it seemed to carry hope, for its effect on Wrack was immediate. With great effort, she relaxed and lifted her head. The poisonous twist of her lips was replaced by a smile.

'Then I must make do with victory,' she said triumphantly.

Turlough was nonplussed. 'How can you win – if there's no wind?' he stuttered.

She looked at him with gloating power. 'My sails can catch the lightest whisper of a breeze. The race is ours. And the prize.'

Striker was beside himself. 'Bosun . . . Bosun . . .' he shouted down the speaking-tube. The helmsman cringed slightly as the Captain flung away from it in fury and strode towards him. But as he reached the man at the wheel, he turned again, and started to pace backwards and forwards, glaring round the empty room.

'Where is everyone?' he ground out. 'Victory is in sight and we idle here! Sails hanging limp!'

The First Mate hurried through the door and he rounded on him explosively. 'Get the men aloft, Mr Marriner! And crack on!'

Marriner did not move. The Doctor and Tegan came slowly in and stood beside him.

' I said "crack on", Mr. Mate,' Striker repeated with quiet fury.

'There's no point.' Marriner said despairingly. 'We just don't have the sail, Captain.'

Striker paced again, this time to look through one of the ports. 'Wrack's pulling away from us!' There was frustration and controlled rage in his voice. 'She's going to win!'

Marriner's head sank and the life seemed to go out of his face. 'We're beaten –' the words died away like an echo. And he stood frozen and immobile again, as he had when Tegan first saw him. Striker, too, seemed to gaze with empty, fixed eyes that saw nothing, not even the ring of harbour lights ahead.

'Beaten?' the word jarred the silence. 'Not quite.' The Doctor's voice was urgent and full of purpose. And as he stepped forward authoritatively, the two Eternals responded, almost as though he had breathed life into them.

'Don't forget Turlough's over there,' he said encouragingly.

Tegan could hardly believe she had heard correctly. 'Turlough!' she repeated contemptuously. 'Him!' How could the Doctor not realise what Turlough was like, she thought. It was pathetic. Turlough was about the last person you could rely on. He was cowardly, selfish, greedy –

'I trust him.' The Doctor's quiet voice broke into her mental catalogue of Turlough's faults. 'He'll stop her.' And then he became brisk and practical again. 'He may need a hand, though.' And turning to Striker and Marriner he went on firmly, 'I shall require my TARDIS.'

The Eternals looked at each other. In some strange way, it was now the Doctor who was the dominant figure in the room. They were like puppets, hanging on his thoughts.

'Very well,' Striker nodded.

Marriner looked into the Doctor's face. 'Concentrate,' he said. The two pairs of eyes locked together, and the stare between them was unblinking and almost hypnotic. Then slowly their eyes closed. They

116

seemed to be in some sort of trance, but the tension in their faces showed the effort involved.

'Where *is* the TARDIS?' Tegan whispered.

'Hidden in the Doctor's mind,' came softly from the Captain.

And then, with its usual grinding, rumbling noise, the TARDIS slowly materialised, right in the middle of the wheel-house. The Doctor opened his eyes. There was enormous relief in them, and for a second, Tegan had a faint idea of just how much the TARDIS meant to him. Then he snapped into action. 'Quickly now, Tegan,' he said briskly. 'No time to waste.' And he made immediately for the door of the transdimensional machine. Tegan followed him, but before they could reach it, Marriner stepped between, and stood, firmly blocking their path.

'Miss Tegan stays with me,' he said.

'No!' the Doctor did not even pause to think.

'She stays. Or you both stay.' There was strength and determination in the young man's face. And, even in her panic, Tegan wondered for a brief minute where the idea had sprung from. Was it from Marriner's own mind? Was he learning again to produce thoughts of his own? But her conjecture was cut short by the Captain's voice.

'Wrack's *running* away from us.'

He stood, staring through the port at the *Buccaneer*, as she crept ahead and the gap between the two ships slowly widened. Tegan felt the same frustration as he did. More than that, she thought suddenly of the White Guardian, and of how important his message had seemed to be.

'Go, Doctor! she said emphatically.

He looked at her, still reluctant, but that simply increased Tegan's determination. She thought of how the Doctor trusted her, of how he had made her co-ordinator once. 'We came here to stop the race. Remember?' she said even more vehemently. 'It'd be silly to fail now! and she almost pushed the Time Lord towards the TARDIS. Marriner stepped aside immediately. The Doctor opened the door and went in. Just before it closed, he gave Tegan one last long worried look, and then the TARDIS was going – going – gone.

'She's almost won!' Striker shouted despairingly. Tegan and Marriner rushed to stare at the screen with him, and the three of them watched with sinking hearts as the *Buccaneer* edged nearer and nearer to the ring of welcoming lights.

'The Doctor will never stop her now!' Striker almost groaned the words.

The TARDIS materialised right by the 'Danger' door. 'Perfect placing,' the Doctor thought briefly, as he hurried out. 'The stay in my mind doesn't seem to have done her any harm. With one quick glance, he took in the 'full power' position of the vacuum shield gauge, and then he opened the door. Wrack was standing in the middle of the grid, facing him. She smiled as she saw him and slowly raised her arms and looked up at the 'eye' above her.

'No! No, wait –' the Doctor called. He did not look to right or left, his whole attention was on Wrack, all his energy concentrated on stopping her before it was too late. Without a second thought he stepped onto the grid and started balancing his way towards her, still talking.

'The power you're tapping – you think it's under your control . . . it isn't . . . it will control *you* . . .'

Wrack slowly shook her head.

'You don't understand what it is!' the Doctor went on desperately. He had almost reached her, when there was a clang, as the door was slammed behind him. He turned. Turlough stood in front of it. Mansell was advancing from the other corner.

'Throw him into the void,' Wrack commanded, her eyes alight with a deadly anticipation.

'Turlough –' The Doctor said the one word and then no more. He stood, swaying precariously over the grid as the two men closed in on him. Wrack watched gloatingly.

'What is the Doctor doing!' The exclamation was wrenched from Tegan, as she watched the screen, practically biting her nails in frenzy. Striker's face was dark and closed, Marriner's held no hope. And then a brief flare of light seemed to shoot from the side of the ship ahead of them. It died in the darkness of space, and another followed.

'What was that?' Tegan asked.

'Man overboard,' Marriner answered, heavily.

It took a second for it to sink in, and then the realisation hit Tegan like a tidal wave. If someone had been thrown from the deck of that ship –

'Not the Doctor! Her voice sounded thin and strange in her own ears. All the objects in the room seemed on a different plane. Reality changed. 'It couldn't be the Doctor!' she heard someone saying, pathetically and she recognised it as her own voice, speaking from miles away.

'The *Buccaneer* is still moving.' Marriner's pronouncement was final, like a mathematician writing Q.E.D. at the end of a problem.

If the Doctor had not succeeded in stopping Wrack, then it must – of necessity – have been his body which

119

was tossed overboard.

'She has not even slackened speed,' Striker's mournful voice added. Proof positive. 'And the second shooting star,' Tegan thought to herself, vaguely, 'Turlough perhaps. Who knows.'

There was a sudden fountain of lights ahead, like fireworks.

'The Doctor has failed,' Marriner said, dully.

'And Wrack has won,' came bitterly from the Captain.

Tegan buried her face in her hands. Slowly, all animation seemed to drain from the faces of the two Eternals, and when Marriner spoke again it was in a flat, dead voice. 'The race is over.' Tegan did not even look up. 'Is the Doctor dead?' she asked, in a mutter thick with tears. 'I don't know,' Striker answered, detachedly. Marriner turned to Tegan. Stiffly he put a hand out and raised her chin, so that he looked into her tear-stained face.

'I see . . . grief,' he said woodenly. 'What is grief?'

Tegan stared ahead, almost as frozen as the Eternals.

'Come, we must cross to Wrack's ship,' she heard Striker's dead voice saying.

'Why?' she sobbed. And she hardly heard the answer, as it died away on Striker's lips.

'Wrack has won. We must pay homage . . .'

She was barely conscious of boarding the launch, or of the crew milling about in confusion as they left. Jackson – Collier – all of them – were like dream figures, and like dreams they suddenly seemed to vanish. As indeed they did, returned to their own times. The same thing happened aboard the *Buccaneer*, – a mad flurry of activity as the crew lost their bearings, panicked, and then came to themselves, perhaps on a square-rigger afloat somewhere in the Caribbean.

Both ships were deserted, mere floating hulks, when the Enlighteners came aboard. In the centre of Wrack's empty stateroom, a figure slowly materialised, robed and cowled. As it shimmered in the air, it seemed to be two figures – identical. They separated, and one of them, with cupped hands, moved to the table. Something was placed there. And when the hands were removed, a small glass dome remained on the wooden boards. It was filled with bright light – so bright, indeed, that both figures were forced to shade their eyes. Then, slowly, the brilliance died.

'Let the victors receive their prize,' said the voice of the White Guardian. One of the Enlighteners pushed back his cowl, and then the other. The two Guardians stood there — of Light and of Darkness.

'You will never destroy the light,' the White Guardian said calmly.

The Black Guardian smiled. 'Others shall do it for me.'

'Destroy the light and you destroy yourself,' the White Guardian went on, as though it was an age-old argument between them. 'Dark cannot exist without knowledge of light.'

'Nor light without dark,' the Black Guardian replied sardonically. And then, as the White Guardian seemed to glimmer slightly, he went on in a jeering voice, 'Your power is waning.'

'Others shall re-charge it for me,' the White Guardian mimicked him.

The Black Guardian laughed. 'These creatures know neither good nor evil,' he said easily. 'Enlightenment will give them power. They will invade Time itself. Chaos will come again. The Universe will

121

dissolve.' The prospect seemed to please him. And then he suddenly called out in a loud voice, 'Where is the Captain of this ship? Where is the Captain to receive the prize?'

The voice that answered made his reverberating tones seem rather over-dramatic. It was normal and reasonable. 'I'm afraid the Captain can't be with us,' it said. And into the room walked the Doctor. 'She met with a rather unfortunate accident,' he said regretfully. 'She fell overboard. So did the First Mate. Thanks to the assistance of my friend here.' Turlough came to stand beside him. 'Although I wasn't sure for a minute which of us you were going to push,' he said softly to the boy. 'Neither was I' was the enigmatic reply. The Doctor looked again at the two Guardians. 'What I meant to say was — with assistance from my friend here — I brought the ship into harbour.'

'You lie!' The Black Guardian roared.

'Oh no!' The Doctor's voice was still gentle and reasonable. 'I leave lies and deception to you,' and he stared back at the menacing figure.

The White Guardian glowed slightly more brightly. 'It seems Enlightenment is yours, Doctor.'

The Time Lord gave him a searching look, then shook his head, almost sadly.

'I'm not ready for it,' came the modest reply. The Whit Guardian glowed more brightly still, and he looked triumphantly in the Black Guardian's direction. 'I don't think anyone is,' the Doctor went on, with regret. 'Especially Eternals.'

The stateroom doors were flung open almost before he had finished speaking, and Striker and Marriner stood there, a small figure between them. It darted forward, to throw its arms round the Doctor in a surprising hug. 'You're alive!' Tegan almost sobbed with delight. The Doctor appeared slightly embarassed by this excess of emotion. 'Shouldn't I be?' he asked casually. But the White Guardian had raised his arms in a dismissing gesture. 'The Ephemeral crews have been returned to their own times. Let the Eternals now return from whence they came.' There was such power in the voice, that nobody demurred. Except for Marriner. He stepped forward with desperation in his eyes. 'No!' he said. 'I want to stay!'

'Back!' said the White Guardian. 'Back to your echoing spaces, where your existence is endless and meaningless. Back to the vastness of eternity.'

Marriner looked at Tegan with pleading in his eyes.

'Help me!' he begged.

Tegan was confused and terrified. She still did not quite understand what was happening. 'I can't,' she answered. But Marriner did not give up easily. 'I need you — I need you —' he called, stretching out his arms to her. 'I need you . . . need you . . .' the calls slowly died away into echoes as he and his Captain faded from view. The last glimmer of them was of Marriner's hand, stretched out towards her.

'There was nothing we could do,' the Doctor said quietly.

Then the White Guardian spoke. 'You were right, Doctor, in judging no one fit to claim all Enlightenment.' His voice suddenly became much more businesslike, — in fact he sounded rather like the Chairman of a large company. 'I can, however, allocate a share,' he said, and looked at Turlough. 'To you.' Turlough gaped. 'Me?' His voice was bewildered.

The White Guardian surveyed him, assessing him. 'You assisted in bringing the ship to harbour,' he announced, and he slowly raised the cover of the glass dome. The light that blazed out was positively blinding, and everyone involuntarily shaded their eyes. Then, slowly as the glare subsided, they could see what lay there! It was a huge diamond, every facet winking with rainbow colours. Turlough stepped forward and looked at it covetously and there was wonder in his voice. 'That size! It'd buy a galaxy.' He shot the White Guardian a look of naked greed. 'You mean — I can have that?' he asked.

'Yes', was the solemn reply.

But just as he was reaching out a hand, the Black Guardian spoke. 'Although, I think I should point out, that in view of the agreement we have I could claim it.'

'This whole thing has become more like a boardroom meeting than ever,' Tegan thought hysterically. But the Black Guardian was going on. 'Unless, of course, you wish to surrender something else in its place.' He looked at the Doctor. So did Turlough. He still had not quite got the point, and the Doctor gave him no help, simply stared impassively ahead.

'The Doctor is in debt to you. For his life,' the Black Guardian continued suavely. And as though addressing a major shareholder, he leaned towards Turlough and said persuasively, 'Give me the Doctor, and you shall have the diamond. You may have the TARDIS as well — anything you wish,' and he waved his hand in an all-encompassing gesture.

Turlough began to imagine what he would do with a gem that size. He could buy anything he wanted. People would listen to him. They would look at him admiringly. They would crawl to him. Nobody would ever bully him again. He would have power.

'Consider, Turlough,' the White Guardian's voice broke in on his thoughts. 'Which will you give up —

this diamond — or the Doctor? The choice is yours.'

He moved the dome towards Turlough.

Nobody would push him around. Nobody would frighten him! He would show them! He was as good as any of them. Turlough had decided. He glanced at the Doctor to see how he was going to take it. The Doctor was simply looking gravely into the middle distance. With that infuriatingly kind expression. Turlough would have liked to kick it in. He hated the Doctor. And then an awful realisation struck him. He *had* to hate the Doctor. He had to make himself. He had known that all along. Otherwise he would never be able to do it. And then what would happen to him! He must not weaken. He must think of himself — look after himself — nobody else would! This was his moment. And then he looked at the Doctor again, and the truth was unavoidable. He liked the Doctor. He admired him. And he would have died rather than go through with it.

'Here! Take it!' Turlough burst out. And he gave the dome and diamond a great shove across the table. The push was so violent, that it was toppling as it slid, and when it arrived at its destination it tipped over completely and crashed. The dome shattered and a blaze of light shone up into the Black Guardian's face.

For a horrible moment he writhed and twisted, then burst into flames. He seemed to contort and dissolve in the heat like a photographic negative. There was a stunned silence, and then the White Guardian got to his feet.

'Light destroys the dark,' he said, as though simply concluding a meeting. 'I think you'll find your contract terminated.'

Turlough did not know what he meant for a minute. Then he pulled the Communication Cube from his pocket. All that remained of it was a blackened, burnt-out shell. He hurled it into the blazing heap on the chair, and the Doctor and Tegan and he watched it, as the flames caught it and blazed up brighter for a moment, and then slowly sank. Before long, all that was left on the chair was a heap of drifting ash.

'I never wanted to make the pact with him,' Turlough said quietly. The Doctor looked at him at last. 'I didn't think so,' he replied gently. Tegan could not stand it any longer. 'You're mad!' she burst out to the Doctor. 'You're not going to believe him? Just because he gave up his share of Enlightenment!'

'He didn't,' the Doctor replied, giving her a long look. 'You've missed the point, Tegan. Enlightenment wasn't the diamond! Simply a lump of carbon! Enlightenment was the choice.'

'Be vigilant!' came the White Guardian's voice, as started to fade. 'The Black Guardian will try again —'

'Hasn't he been destroyed?', Turlough asked, in a bewildered voice. He could not believe that any creature had survived that holocaust. But though the White Guardian's voice was fainter still, he heard the reply. 'While I exist, he exists. Until we are no longer needed.' And then he was gone.

Tegan looked round the deserted wheel-house. Its outlines were blurring and becoming indistinct, as though the matter of which it was composed was becoming tenuous, was slowly starting to dissolve; as though soon the whole ship, like officers and crew, would disappear and only space remain. 'Can't we get away from here?' she asked with a shudder.

'Anywhere in particular?' The Doctor was practical as always.

'My home planet.' There was a great longing in Turlough's voice, and the Doctor looked at him sympathetically. 'Why not? he said, with a smile. 'The TARDIS is waiting.'